I0538732

ALEX

Copyright © 2022

Kathe Olafson and Richard Koreen

Canadian Cataloging in Publication Data
Alex / Richard, Kathe
ISBN 978-0-9949633-4-5

Front and back cover art, layout and design
by Richard Koreen

image sources:
front cover - storm scene - pixabay.com 5962270
back cover - rocky point - pixabay.com 3456582

ALEX

KATHE RICHARD

published by:

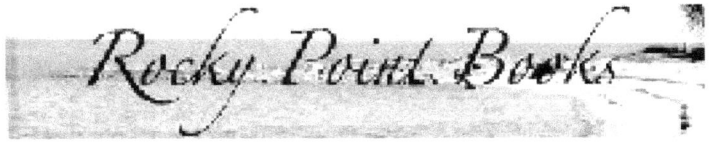

Rocky Point Books

Box 424 Gimli MB CA R0C 1B0

RockyPointBooks@icloud.com

authors may be contacted through the publisher

iii

Also by Kathe Olafson and Richard Koreen:

as Kathe Richard

After Sigga

by Richard Koreen

Feel the Spirit of this Place

by Kathe Olafson

Just Scratch the Surface

This book is dedicated to our patient spouses
Diane and Brian

We are indebted to our readers
Ishbel Moore, Jaime Bouw, Diane Koreen, Brian Olafson,
Brendan Koreen, John Burstow

ALEX
Table of Contents

Chapter...

ALEX

Chapter One — Alexander

July 1950

The sun beats down on Alexander's coal black hair. He works his digger's shovel into the sand, lifts the load, "RRRRRRRR...RRRRRRRR," swings, "kachung... kachung," and dumps, "shshshshsh," overflowing his new Tonka truck. "Hey Joe, got a big load for ya." Alex pushes his truck, spreading a wake. "Move over Joe, let me through." He pushes his truck around Joe, tips the dump and pours the sand on the flattened spot. "See. A load for Joe...don't ya know...ho, ho, ho." His face lights up. "It sounds the same. Load for Joe...don't ya know...ho, ho, ho." He laughs and looks at his friend. Joe sits, downcast. "This is your part Joe, you get to build the house." Joe looks back at him, angry, a bit sad.

Alex says, "What's wrong? You want a turn with the truck?" Joe nods.

"Okay you get a turn." He stands and watches Joe do a load. "Good job Joe. Look at him go, my friend Joe." Alex laughs and takes his turn.

Richard stands at the kitchen sink watching his son through the window. *What a kid! He seems happy. Not a care in the world. He'll do okay. Does that make what I have to do easier?* He shakes his head and a blonde strand slips onto his forehead. He turns and looks at Ruby, sitting at the kitchen table with her constant companions, a cigarette and coffee. He watches her blood red nails mindlessly tap the coffee cup. *She's so thin her fingers look like claws.* He closes his eyes to rid himself of the image. *What a mess I'm in. God help me...I can't do this anymore, I have to make things right. Alexander? He's a sweet little boy and Ruby'll look after him. Of course she will.*

He looks back out at the sandbox. *He looks nothing like me. No one in my family has that nose, or hair that dark.* He looks back to Ruby. *Well, there's the nose, and she might have dark hair under that red dye. Is he really mine? He looks nothing like me...no, that's just me looking for an easy way out. Whatever. I need to end this now.*

His sleeve brushes an encrusted bowl off the pile in the sink. It hits the floor and shatters. *Shit! This place's a pig sty.* He bends down and carefully picks up the pieces. *How can I leave Alexander to this...* He takes a deep breath. *No. Can't think like that. This has to end.* He places the pieces in the overflowing kitchen trash, turns and asks, "Who's Alex talking to?"

Ruby snorts. "His imaginary friend, Joe. Idiot. He talks to him all the time."

"But he's alone."

"He's an imaginary friend, Alex calls him Joe. He plays with him all the time."

"Should you be concerned? Does he need help?"

"Talked with other moms, one of them's a teacher and they say it's a stage. Just a thing kids go through."

"So nothing to worry about?"

"Right."

2

"Alex's five this month, starts Kindergarten this fall, right?"

Ruby tips a dash of whiskey into her coffee and looks up. "Yeah, I'll enroll him soon."

Richard sighs. "Ruby, we have to talk. This just isn't working anymore. It's time for me to move on."

Her body tenses. "What!?"

"I've got my family to think about. Kathe and the new baby are my family now. This has run its course and…"

"Kathe and the new baby! What about Alex? What about you and me? We have something special between us." Her face hardens. "We aren't good enough anymore? I get it. Alexander's a bastard and I'm your whore."

"You know I don't think like that."

"Well, he is a bastard and you're married to Kathe and that makes me the other woman, a whore. So in your nice little world, how does 'moving on' look?"

"It's been good but it's time for me to grow up and become responsible. I really haven't been fair to my wife. Of course, I'll take care of you and Alex."

Ruby butts her cigarette, steps over and pushes her body into his, her face close. "So you'll be around less often."

"No, I won't be around at all. It's over."

Ruby wraps her arms around Richard's neck. "C'mon Honey you know we're good together." She grinds her hips against him and pulls his head down towards her lips.

Richard pushes her away. "No. Not now. Not again."

"You bastard!" She swings at his face.

He catches her wrist and squeezes it. She winces as he says firmly, "Get this straight, we are done."

Ruby puts on her lustful smile and croons, "No you don't mean it. No one will ever do the things I do for you. You'll be

3

back here for real sex. We know each other, we need each other." She pushes against him but Richard steps away.

"You're wrong. I do mean it, we're done… I'll take care of you. I've spoken with my lawyer. This house'll be yours and you'll get a generous lump sum. You'll be okay."

"I don't want your money. I want you. What the hell happened?"

"The baby happened. Kathe and I are a family now…This fling is over…I've been a jerk."

"But you love me. You know you love me."

Damn, I didn't want to say this. "No Ruby. I don't love you." *I hate myself.*

Ruby yells, "Yes you do. Every time we make love you tell me you love me."

He shakes his head. "No, I told you I love the things you do when we have sex. It never was lovemaking, just sex. Damn good sex, but there's more to life."

"You bastard." Ruby sits, puts her head on her arms and pretends to cry. She thinks, *God, I knew this would happen someday, but not yet. I'm not ready. Damn it. Think. There must be a way.*

She lifts her head, the one tear she has manufactured rolls down her cheek. "What about Alexander? What about him? You can't just walk away from him."

"I'm going to have to. The two of you will be just fine with the house and money."

Her face twists as she snarls, "Really, just like that you think you can buy me off. Well think again mister. I'll make your life miserable. I will. Your precious Kathe'll dump you when I get finished."

"Ruby, you listen. The house and money come with a non-disclosure agreement. Say anything to anybody at any time

4

and you lose it all. My lawyer will be down this weekend to get your signature on the papers. If you don't sign them I'll take my chances that Kathe will understand and not leave me. I will not be blackmailed."

Ruby slumps in her chair.

"Do you understand?"

"Yes, damn it. It better be worth my while, you shit. You fucking asshole. Get out!" she yells, "I can't stand being near you. Get out!"

He hesitates.

She picks up the whiskey bottle and fills her cup. He opens the kitchen door and steps into the back yard.

Alex looks up and smiles. "Thanks for the great truck, Daddy." The smile fades as he anxiously asks, "Mommy's yelling?"

Richard leans down and pats his head.

"You're a good boy, Alex. I got you something for your treasure box. You still have the cigar box I gave you, right? For your treasures?"

"Yup. Keep all my lucky stones and stuff in it. It's a great box. Just for my stuff."

Richard takes a magnet out of his shirt pocket and shows Alex.

"What's that Daddy?"

"It's a magnet. Here, I'll show you how it works." He pulls out his pocket knife, opens it. "See the metal attracts the magnet and it won't fall off." He shakes it gently.

Alex looks at the knife, eyes wide. "Wow. Cool knife. Can I hold it?"

"No son, you're too young. It's my old Boy Scout jackknife. See this, it's got a fleur-de-lis, the Boy Scout emblem."

5

"Fleur-de-lis, happy like me." He smiles at the music his words make. "That's a cool knife, Daddy. Can I get one?"

"Maybe someday." Richard hesitates, trying to find the right words. "Alex I'm going away for a while and I want you to be a good boy for your mom."

"Okay. Gotcha. Thanks for the maggot."

Richard smiles. "Magnet, it's called a magnet. It's got a 'nnn' sound in the middle."

"Okay, gotcha, magnet." He turns back to his truck, swings another load of dirt and dumps it into his shiny Tonka. Richard squats, watches as Alex makes five more trips with his truck, burying the flat spot, and then parks beside the sandbox construction site. "That's all we can do today Joe. The other workers will come and make the walls."

Richard, hating himself, stands and pats Alex's head. "Remember — Try your best to be your best."

Alexander smiles as his Dad's hand touches his head. *Try my best...to be my best. That's good, sounds the same, like a song.* Richard walks slowly away. At the gate he looks back one more time. *At least he has his friend Joe.*

Seeing his Dad leaving, Alex jumps up and says, "C'mon Joe,"C'mon Joe, we're pilots. Let's wave to Daddy." Spreading his arms, he runs through the side yard, out the gate and into the street. "Wave, Joe. Wave." The two friends wave as Richard's car disappears down the road. Alexander runs up and down the street weaving, flying high, swooping low. "We're fighter pilots! Bullets! brabrabrabrabra! We're hit! Parachute!" Alex runs and jumps onto the fence. "C'mon Joe, we'll jump off." Joe looks worried. Alex shrugs and jumps off, pulling his pretend ripcord. "We're okay Joe!" He jumps back on. "Don't be a scaredy cat! We have the funnest fence."

6

'Crack!' Half the fence wavers, then collapses. *Oh, oh.* Horrified, Alex looks at the broken fence, then at the house.

Joe looks at Alex and the fence, slowly shakes his head.

"Let's go Joe. We'll go to our spot." They walk down South Colonization Road arm in arm heading toward McCurdy's equipment shed. In behind, next to the derelict tractor they sit down and Alex says, "Come on Joe. Let's make a plan."

Late in the afternoon Alex drags his feet, stomach growling as he passes the downed fence. "You'll come in with me, won't you Joe?" Joe stops at the sidewalk and shakes his head. Alex pulls on his arm. "C'mon be a friend." Joe reluctantly follows.

Ruby stands in the middle of the living room, her auburn hair fallen out of its ponytail and her makeup caked and streaked. Her shoulders sag, in her left hand dangles an almost empty whiskey bottle.

Ruby's bleary eyes swing towards her son and she slurs, "We're just not good enough…but he's gonna help us. Right!" *God, he did say he loved me…* She looks back into the kitchen…"To hell with his help." Ruby lifts the bottle to her lips and winces as the last ounce burns her throat. "Whadaya want. There's nothing here for you. Go play outside." She breaks the seal on another bottle. *Ten thousand times he said, 'I love you'.*

"Mommy I'm hungry…"

"Get out!" *Wonder if he ever meant it…maybe once. Then he screws God damned Kathe…and this time out pops Steven…the end of us.*

The boys turn and run into the back yard. They sit on the swing and rock back and forth. Alex looks over at the sand

7

box. "I'm so hungry. You hungry Joe? It's been a long time since breakfast...Hey, where's my truck?"

The kitchen screen door bursts open and Ruby staggers onto the stoop.

Alex looks at her, then to the side for Joe. He's not there. He confronts his mom alone. "Hey Mom, my truck's gone."

"Yeah, it's gone. I'll get you a good truck. From me, someone who loves you."

Puzzled, Alex asks, "Where is it?"

Ruby sways, turns around and goes back into the kitchen. Alex yells after her, "You gettin' it?"

In the kitchen Ruby looks at the smashed remains of the toy dump truck. *So I went a little bit nuts...Richard is an asshole...I needed to hit something.*

Behind her a small voice says, "Mommy, my truck. What happened to my truck?"

Ruby blinks and carefully says, "Well, Mommy had a little accident. But don't worry, we'll get you a better truck. Mommy is sorry, okay?"

Alex shifts from foot to foot. "A bigger one?"

"Yes, the biggest and bestest one. But tomorrow okay? Mommy has to lie down now. You go outside and play until the street lights come on."

Alexander runs outside, jumps over the fence lying in the yard and heads to the lake. He looks back and Joe appears. "Hey c'mon, we'll go to the beach and..." Joe shakes his head. Alex laughs and runs off. Joe reluctantly follows. Up and down the beach they search, selecting only the best shells. "See Joe, the best ones have no breaks, no holes, just shell. This one's perfect, best yet. I'll put it in the box with my other good stuff. And Daddy's maggot too."

Alex is almost down to Betel Retirement Home when the street lights flicker to life. His shoulders slump. "Okay Joe, we gotta go home. Hope Mom's quit drinking." Alex thinks, *Don't get good shells every day. I got, let's see.* He holds them in both hands and counts, stacks them, stuffs them into his pocket. "Leventy seven. Good haul, eh Joe?" And they walk side by side along the beach.

At the front door Alex yells, "Hi Mom. What's for supper?" He stops, dismayed.

A very drunk Ruby confronts him, slurring, "Don't 'Hi Mom' me, you little bastard, it's all your fault." She shifts her weight to her other foot and loses her balance, grabs the couch arm to steady herself. "It's all your fault." She falls into the couch, arches her back and throws up on the front of her sweater. Alex recoils at the sight and smell.

"Don't hit me Mom. It just fell over. It can be fixed. I'll fix it tomorrow."

Ruby wipes her mouth and tries to focus. "What the hell you talking about?"

"The fence. I just touched it and it fell."

"I'm talking about your Daddy. He's gone and he's not coming back and it's all your fault. You're never good enough. He loves his new baby more, 'cause we're just no good. Steven is better, you're no good."

"Mommy…"

"No good I tell you. You're just no good." Ruby passes out into the mess on the couch.

Alexander bursts into tears...*I'm no good, I'm no good...Daddy left...I didn't do my best to be my best...* Alexander falls to the floor, grabs his knees and curls into a ball. He begins shaking. Between sobs he says, "Hug me Joe. Be my friend, hug me." Alex pants as he sobs, desperately asks, "Where are you Joe? I need you."

9

Chapter Two — Alexander is Smitten

August 1958

Thirteen year old Alex follows a hearse slowly down Third Avenue to the Lutheran Church. He stands quietly beside his bike and watches two men open the back door of the vehicle. "Wow! Look Joe, we're gonna see a dead body." Joe shivers, but Alex, fascinated, drops his bike and sits on the grass to watch. Joe stands beside him, apprehensive. The men maneuver the coffin onto a trolley, push it up the sidewalk and disappear into the church. "Aw gee, that's nothing…still, there's a dead body in the box." He starts to stand but sits back down as more cars arrive.

A car with out-of-province plates stops in front of the Church. Three solemn adults exit and file up the walk. The car moves off. Alex follows it with his eyes as it slowly, deliberately parks. Meanwhile, a gray car has pulled in. From it a girl in a light blue dress and her black-clad mother get out. They stand waiting as the driver parks the car. He joins them, straightens his black tie and together they proceed up the walk. The girl's dress catches the light and shimmers.

Alexander is mesmerized by the vision. *She's pretty. Prettiest girl I've ever seen.* The sun backlights her hair. *It's a golden halo.* She skips a step and Alex's heart skips a beat. *She's so beautiful.* He sighs as she disappears into the church.

"Wow! Did you see that Joe? She's like a doll in a catalogue, or a princess. No, she's an angel…My Angel. Who is she? I've never seen her before. She's a cool chick…my new girl, yeah, she's my new girl…My Angel. Whatcha think Joe? She's cool?" An impulse ripples across his groin. He scrunches his penis and testicles in his hand and a look of wonder crosses his face. *My Perfect Angel, come with me, forever happy we will be.* He sits entranced, watching. Enjoying the image, he quietly murmurs, "Golden, shiny, soft, pretty, angel…"

A black sedan pulls up, jarring him back to the present, he holds his breath as Richard Oddleifson, his wife and their son Steve get out and head up the walk. "Look Joe, there's my Dad." He whispers, "Dad, look over here…here I am. Look at me! Joe, make him look at me. I'm here. Can't you see I'm here? Joe help me!" He stops. Joe puts his arm around him and Alex's face crumples, his pulse quickens. "It's me, Dad. See me? I wish you'd look at me. I'm being my best." Dejected, Alex looks around for Joe but he's gone. Alex lays down and curls up on the grassy boulevard. "Where are you Joe? Hug me. Be a friend, hug me."

Alex pedals furiously, almost keeping up with the funeral cortege as it wends its way to the cemetery. *Where'd Joe go? Who's the dead guy ? Who's that woman? Why's she and Dad at the funeral?* He overtakes the line of cars on the bumpy trail into the grave yard and lays his bike down beside a tombstone. He crouches behind a shrub and peers across the ditch at the hearse waiting as the cars slowly pull up and park.

Finally, the limo opens. Richard and his family get out, followed by the Angel and her parents. *She must be part of the family! Steve's standing beside her and holding her hand. I'm gonna kill him! He can't have my Angel. I hate him! Let go of my girl! You can't have her!*

One after another the cars open and silent mourners walk to the grave and stand, waiting. The coffin is removed from the back of the hearse and carried to the grave. They lay it on

11

the belts and step back. The Pastor intones, waves his hand over the grave and Alex hears, "…dust to dust…" and the casket lowers slowly. Everyone stands very still for several moments and then the back row starts to quietly drift off. Soon only Richard, Steve and the Angel with her mother are standing graveside.

Alex's bike meanders on North Colonization Road. *So, that was my Dad and that bastard Steve. My Angel...he held her hand, but she's mine, my Angel...how does she fit in? How's her mom fit in?...My Angel, pretty, my prettiest Angel.* The impulse in his groin! He grabs his crotch. His bike wobbles to the roadside, he hops off and sits in the ditch, panting, wondering.

He rests and calms down, then heads downtown towards the dock. *God, I'm hungry. What else is new? Mom has to start feeding me. I can't...It's her!* He spies his Angel and her mother walking into Tergesen's General Store. He stands his bike against the wall and walks in behind them. He ducks behind displays but keeps them in sight. They look around but don't buy anything. He watches them leave and head down the street to Tip Top Grocery. He follows and stares through the window at them. He stands still, dreaming. His face goes slack as he imagines talking to his Angel. A goofy smile spreads across his face. The mother is gesturing to the man behind the meat counter but stops when she sees Alex in the window. Frowning, she turns and talks to her daughter.

The pair exit Tip Top and walk down First Avenue. Every once in a while the mother turns and frowns at the strange boy closely following them.

"Do you know that boy?"

"No Mommy, he looks older."

"He keeps staring at us. I saw him at Tip Top. Have you seen him before?"

12

"No, I don't think so."

"He's following us."

Alex can't take his eyes off her. *She's beautiful.* He feels the familiar ripple in his groin. He gazes into space and his mouth falls open.

The mother becomes uncomfortable. "There's something wrong with that boy. Come Sigga, we're leaving."

"But I'm hungry."

"We're leaving. We'll eat when we get back to Winnipeg. Now let's find your father."

Alex hears the mother. *Her name's Sigga. My Angel Sigga. Her mother said there's something wrong with me. Wrong with me? No, I'm a good boy. Nothing wrong with me...*

Alex grabs his bike, races down South Colonization Road and turns in at McCurdy's equipment shed. He lies between the shed and the derelict tractor and breathes slowly, deeply. *What's she mean there's something wrong with me. I'm a good boy.* Joe appears on the grass beside him. "Where've you been? I needed you." Joe smiles and sits closer. "That woman said there's something wrong with me." A mouse scampers onto a clump of grass and stops, looks at him. With a flick of his wrist he grabs it and holds it in his hand. His breathing slows and the events of the day slip from him. He lies very still.

Angel Sigga, I love you
Angel Sigga, we are two
Stand by me and we will see
Our perfect love eternally

13

Angel Sigga, I love you — he strokes the rodent with his finger

Angel Sigga, you are soft —

His father's face appears and tension builds. *Daddy, why can't you see me? Why can't you love me? I'm a good boy. I do my best to be my best*...The mouse squirms, Alex increases the pressure, there's a small noise and his fist collapses. Bloody liquid oozes between his fingers and down his forearm. Alex feels strong. He clenches his teeth and fills his lungs to bursting. His eyes bulge and energy surges through him. His father's face disappears.

Chapter Three — Alex Gets the Missing Pieces

Elated, Alex looks at the traces of blood on his hand and pedals madly. "Joe. I'm free! I've never felt this before, I'm free." He remembers the mouse squirming in his hand and picks up speed. "I feel…powerful, yeah, powerful! Screw him! Screw that bastard! I don't need him. C'mon Joe." He jumps off his bike, walks into the house and yells, "Mom." Joe lags behind cautiously but slips in as the door is closing, then sees Ruby slumped in her chair at the kitchen table and disappears.

"Stop screaming for Christ's sake. I've got such a head." Ruby tries to focus. Dark brown roots now support the carefully dyed red hair, lines are etched around her mouth. "What're you doing home? It's not dinner yet." She wraps her hand around the bottle on the table and splashes a drink into her glass.

Alex washes the dried ooze off his hands in the kitchen sink and looks at the bottle. *Two thirds full. She's not slurring. Must be her first bottle. Not too drunk yet, maybe I can ask her about the old guy's funeral.*

He sits down across from her and says, "Mom I was at the church, there was a big funeral. It was huge. Cars parked everywhere. Musta been someone important."

Ruby smirks, sits up straighter and looks at Alex. "Oh yeah it was someone important alright. Too goddamned important for the likes of us."

Alex looks closely at her. "You know who I saw there?"

Ruby looks back at him, irritated. "I can guess who you saw there. That no good father of yours, right?"

Alex nods. "Why was he there Mom? Is he related to the dead guy?"

Ruby throws back her drink and grabs the bottle, pours another and yells, "Goddamn Gunnar Oddleifson was his father. The sainted Gunnar Oddleifson with a big stick up his ass. Too good for the likes of us." Her neck veins stand out, her face flushes, she sucks in her breath.

"Ah Mom don't get so upset. I'm sorry I asked."

Ruby snorts. "Yeah you're sorry, you should be...you should see what you don't got...what we don't get. Damn it. Then you'll be sorry, really sorry." She reaches for her car keys.

"Mom you can't drive. Remember what the cops said last time."

"Shut up. Get in the car. You're gonna see what should be ours. What we lost. What I lost." She turns on Alex and through her teeth angrily hisses, "It's all your fault."

Alex holds on as Ruby leans through an abrupt turn onto Highway 231. All the while Ruby rants, "Goddamned Oddleifsons! Too good for li'l ol' Ruby Gislason. Right! Bastards, all of them."

Geez what've I done. "Mom slow down. You don't want the cops..."

"Shut up. Listen and learn, kid. We should've been at that funeral. Me and your dad and you...a family...but 'No', we're not good enough. Goddamned Oddleifsons. Think they're better than anyone else."

"Shit!" Ruby slams on the breaks. Alex lurches forward. She throws the car into reverse and backs up, turns onto a side road. She floors it and the tires throw gravel wildly behind. A few minutes down the road she stops. Both sides of the road

16

are lined with cars. "I see all the righteous in town are here to pay their respects and kiss ass...Look at that, kid."

Mouth agape, Alex looks at a sprawling house with a paved drive lined with flower beds. *The grass is like a green carpet. Wow! Just like a house on TV.*

"See that, kid? And the land, that's all Oddleifson land. Miles and miles of money. Should be ours. Should be mine." She starts crying, stops as an idea forms, says slyly, "Now I'm going to show you something else. Hold on tight, kid."

She makes a left turn back onto 231, all the time muttering under her breath, "Yeah, I'll show you where it all began."

Alex has a mind full of questions but stays quiet. *So, is the dead guy my grandfather? But what about my Angel Sigga? Is it her grandfather too? Can't be.*

Ruby makes a gravel spewing turn onto Burma Road. She's laughs maniacally. "Yeah, this is where it all began. Stupid me! This is where you began you little bugger. Now where is that road? It's around here somewhere. I guess no one comes here much now. Ah, this is it."

Alex looks around. *Doesn't look like a road to me.* They bounce down an overgrown path, turn behind some bushes and stop in front of a rundown shack. "Look Alex. The old Oddleifson homestead. This is where you started life."

Alex stands in the deep grass. "Looks like an old shack to me. How could I start here?"

Ruby laughs. "You'll know someday. God, wish I'd brought my booze. Yup, this is the wonderful place your dad would bring me back in the day. He used it for hunting. Doesn't look like anybody comes here for anything anymore. I thought I was so smart. Thought he loved me. Yeah, right. No one loves me, never will."

She returns to the car and rummages in her purse. "Here, this's for you. It's me and Richard right here. You're an Oddleifson. You just don't get the stuff that goes with it... Steve gets that." She hands Alex an old, creased photo, looks at him and her eyes narrow, her face hardens. "It's all your fault you little bastard." She lifts her hand to her face and starts sobbing, her self pity overwhelms her, fills her. Her sobs wrack her body.

The emotions flow over Alex. He can hardly breathe. He sucks in a deep breath, says, "Mom lets go. It's time to go." Ruby keeps sobbing and he becomes desperate. He firmly says, "Mom, your booze. Your booze is on the table at home. Let's go."

Ruby quits crying, focuses. "Yeah my booze. Let's go get my booze."

Hours later, Alex pulls the dirty sheet up under his chin and looks at the ceiling. *I'm hungry. She must have passed out by now, wonder if it's safe yet. God what a bitch. Everything's my fault. I didn't ask to be born. I'm so tired of being screamed at, no food, no love.* Alex sneers. *Love! Who am I kidding?...This isn't right.*

Steve sure lucked out. He's got it all...he's got my dad...a family, bet he's had supper. Geez he even has my Angel Sigga. Damn. What do I get? I'm so hungry...I'm going out there. There must be something to eat. She bought a new bottle, maybe she bought some Pop Tarts. Yeah Pop Tarts.

His mother is passed out on the living room floor beside an empty whiskey bottle. Alex looks at her and feels Joe at his side. "Look at her Joe. What a mess! What am I gonna do? I'm so tired." Alex slips his arms under her and lifts. *She's so light. And so drunk.* Her feet drag the threadbare carpet on the

18

short trip to the couch. He lays her down full length, stands back. *She used to be so beautiful…She's a wreck.*

She stirs and looks up at him and mumbles. "You're no good. It's all your fault." She closes her eyes.

Alex starts crying and bends over her. "I'm just a kid. You're my mother. Why can't you be a mother? I'm hungry." His voice gets louder through his tears, "Did you hear me? I'm hungry. Why can't you just be my mother?"

Ruby rouses again and slurs, "Get away from me you useless bastard. You're just a bastard. It's all your fault. All your fault." She pushes back with both arms, trying to get up. Her arm slips and she falls hard between the seat cushions and the back. Her arms are pushed forward. She's wedged in solid, she can't move. Her body convulses and she starts vomiting. She blows the putrid fluid out of her mouth and is about to suck air back in when another spasm wracks her body. Her mouth fills and her lungs are empty. Panic contorts her face. She looks up at her son.

"You're a useless mother," he yells into her panicked face, "Why can't you be a mother? I'm your kid. You're supposed to be the mother. I never asked to be born." Ruby desperately writhes, her stomach churning out noxious vomit. "You're a useless mother." Alex reaches out and grabs her shoulders. Joe stops him. Alex pauses and looks at his friend, then back at his mother. Her eyes, filled with panic lock onto her son. He pulls and his hands slip off her vomit slick flesh.

Alex says to Joe, "She could die." Joe nods solemnly. Alex looks at him and for one second imagines life without her. Joe nods and smiles. Alex mumbles, "It'd be forever." He hesitates, wipes away his tears. "Yes, she could die." He takes a step back. Ruby writhes and arches her back. Alex yells, "You're a useless mother." One last spasm sucks the vomit

19

into her lungs...her thrashing becomes wild, slows, then stops. Joe disappears.

Alex stands looking down at his still mother. *I'm free! Really free. Now I'm really free!*

He pulls her head up a bit and looks closely at her. He takes off one of her fancy blue earrings, *always liked these,* and puts it in his pocket.

The next morning Ruby is still dead, still rammed tightly into the couch, definitely dead. Alex phones the RCMP. *I should be sad, but I'm free.*

The police arrive and the whole process flows around Alex. Ruby's body is lifted onto a gurney and a lady from Social Services stands silently beside him. An RCMP constable writes in his notebook as he looks over the scene. Alex thinks, *I could do that,* then smiles slightly and stands a bit taller. The constable looks at him, finishes a note and slips the book into his uniform breast pocket. Inside Alex's head his mother's voice echoes. ***This is all your fault.*** He looks at the Social Services lady. *She didn't hear anything...* His mother continues, ***You're a useless bastard...useless.*** Alex's eyes fill with fear.

Chapter Four — Alex is Placed

August 1958

Robert MacDonald steers his car carefully around potholes in the road. Alex sees his caseworker's mouth moving but hears no words. His mind is cycling through many unspoken questions. *He doesn't look like he graduated university. How old is this guy? Where're we going? Why can't I stay in my house? Mom's not really dead, she's right here in my head all the time. How can she be here and dead?* Inside his head Ruby says, ***You got that right. Right here with you forever.*** Robert's voice penetrates, "Alex. Are you listening to me?"

Alex turns towards the voice. "Yes sir." He watches Robert press a stocky leg lightly on the brake as he manoeuvres around another hole. *It's funny, you wouldn't know he was so short when he's sitting.*

"We're almost at Mr Freeman's house. You'll like him. He's a retired school teacher and he takes in foster kids."

Retired teacher! Can't be good. ***Good enough for you, you bastard. All you deserve.***

"I need you to be respectful and do what he says. Will you do that?" Alex nods. Robert pulls to the curb and parks. "This is it."

Alex looks out at a small bungalow, white with red trimmed windows. It has a manicured yard surrounded by a short white fence. A slight, grey haired man stands on the porch smiling and waving. Robert and Alex get out of the car and approach. Alex winces as Ruby snarls, ***An old geezer. All you deserve. Good enough for you, you little bastard.***

"Hi George, this is Alex. Alex this is Mr Freeman."

21

"Hi Alex. Call me George. Welcome to your new home." He turns, opens the door and motions for them to enter. Alex cautiously walks up the stairs and as he crosses the threshold, is hit with a wonderful aroma. *What's that? I've never smelled anything like it.* Salivating, he looks around the orderly living room trying to locate the heavenly smell. Behind him Robert laughs. "You're baking bread again George. Sure hope you're planning on sharing."

"Robert, I hope you're staying for lunch. We're going to build man sized sandwiches to welcome my new friend. Alex, come with me, I'll show you your room."

Alex follows him down the hallway taking in as much as he can as they go. *It's so clean. And warm. Maybe this'll be okay.* His room is small but perfectly set up with a red bedspread on the twin bed. A pristine white sheet is folded over the top of the cover, a desk sits under the window with a small pile of books and a globe of the world on one corner. *Just like on TV.* A warmth spreads throughout his body and Ruby is silent. George interrupts his thoughts. "The bathroom is across the hall if you want to wash up before lunch. Come out when you're ready. By the way, do you like canasta?"

Alex looks at him as if he's speaking another language. "Something to eat?"

George laughs. "It's a card game and I'm addicted to it. I'm going to have fun teaching you. Take your time. Come out for lunch when you're ready."

Alex sits down on the bed and looks around. *Am I dreaming? This is great. Wow! Should I get comfortable? Could be too good to be true...I guess we'll see.*

22

February 1960

Alex watches the snow fall gently, then turns to his bed. He opens the lid of his cigar box, three excellent shells, five lucky stones, a magnet, his mother's blue earring. He holds the earring in his palm, looks at it and takes a slow breath. *She was pretty, impossible, a bit nuts, but pretty.* He drops it back in the box and picks up a smooth lucky stone. *Like this one, you can see right through.* He holds it up to his eye and looks into the hole, smiles, puts it back. *So Mom's really dead, and so's George. Heart attack, so fast...one moment, then...* Alex puts the two canasta decks in the box. *Getting a bit tight.* He selects the one perfect shell and discards the other two. *It's okay, I'll be fifteen this summer, I can get rid of kid stuff.* Joe appears beside him, puts his hand on his shoulder. Alex says, "Thanks Joe, you're a good friend."

He puts the cigar box atop the folded clothes in his suitcase and slowly closes the lid. He sits perfectly still on his bed, tears fill his eyes. *You aren't a crybaby. So the old man's dead. So what.* A pair of tears slide down his nose. Pushing them away, he closes his eyes. *He was a great old guy and now he's gone too.* His body jerks gently in rhythm with his sobs. *Why'd he have to die? Now what's gonna happen to me? Shit! Why'd he have to die?* Inside his head Ruby taunts, ***You'll get what you deserve, nothing. A big fat nothing.***

Robert MacDonald calls from the living room, "Ready Alex?"

Alex wipes his eyes, stands, looks around the room one last time, picks up his suitcase and walks dejectedly to the living room. Robert asks, "Ready?" Alex nods.

Robert talks as they exit the house, "Okay, I think I've got a great placement for you. It's on a farm north of town. The

23

Strongs have two grown sons. It's a good place for a kid. Once the snow leaves you'll have acres and acres to run around in."

Alex nods and gets in the car. Robert hands him a business card. "This is my number. Get in touch with me anytime you want, any concerns, anything at all, you can call me. Got that?"

Alex nods but all he sees is the little white house and the old man that waved and smiled at him when he arrived. Ruby interrupts, *He's dead, good riddance. Stupid old man.* Alex looks around for Joe. *That little runt's gone. It's only me now, you useless bastard.*

September 1960

Robert MacDonald races into Emergency. He shows his identification and asks for Alexander Gislason. The nurse looks up and says, without smiling, "The doctor would like to speak to you before you see Alex."

Robert takes a deep breath. "What happened? I got a call to get down here and…"

The nurse sternly raises her hand stopping him. "You'll have to talk to the doctor. Have a seat." She points at the row of chairs.

He sits, watching anxiously down the hallway.

Twenty long minutes pass, then a white coated man approaches. Robert stands to meet him.

"Mr MacDonald?"

"Yes Doctor. Please tell me what's going on?"

"I'm Dr Habib, come in here where we can talk in private."

24

Once settled in a consultation room, the doctor's face grows hard. He looks sharply at Robert and says, "What we're dealing with here is a serious case of classic child abuse. Have you not been checking on this kid? I fail to see how this could have occurred with regular checks."

Robert is taken aback at the tone. "What? Of course I checked. I did my regular visits. Everything was fine every time. You know we are understaffed and overworked but I try my best to stay on top of my caseload. What're we talking about here? What happened?"

The doctor explains in a matter-of-fact manner, "Alexander was brought in with a broken arm. Broken in two places. While the technician was x-raying he noticed a lot of bruising on Alex's shoulders, some new and some old. When questioned, Alexander was very evasive. The Tech was suspicious and when helping him into a hospital gown, observed similar bruising on the buttocks, legs and back. Alexander is closed up and not talking now. He's very thin, almost to the point of malnutrition." He continues angrily, "I cannot see how you could have missed this."

Robert squirms in his chair. "Well he's a teenager, I thought he was just having a growth spurt. I swear he never said a thing to me. God, this is awful. I feel terrible. Can I see him?"

"Yes, I don't have to tell you how to proceed, do I? Slow and careful. No telling how traumatized he is."

Robert looks at Alex through the door window. He is horrified to see how thin and pale he has become. *God help me, when did I last see him? How could I have missed this?* He takes a deep breath and enters the room.

25

Alex sits quietly on a gurney silently counting the floor tiles. He recoils as Robert pulls up a chair. "Alex I'm so sorry. I don't know how this happened." Alex turns his head away. "Why didn't you call me? And when I was there you never said a thing. I'm trying to understand here."

Alex continues to stare off into space. *You left me in hell, man. You don't care. No one cares about me. I'm alone and I guess I always will be. You're all useless. Even Joe's gone.* He cringes as his mother's voice screams in his head. ***Useless, useless, you're useless. No one loves you. Useless. Useless. Useless.*** *Yeah, I'm on my own, except for her...Shit!*

Chapter Five — Steve is Careless

June 1961

"Geez guys, come on, this isn't funny. Who took it? C'mon Benny!" Steve Oddliefson looks at his friend. Benny looks back at him bewildered. Steve turns to Ralph. "Okay, give it back."

Another gobsmacked face looks back at him. "You guys didn't take it?" Two heads simultaneously shake back and forth. Steve grabs a hand full of his sandy hair and pulls, looks around frantically.

Ralph says, "It was right there. In the trunk right below mine. I saw it. Then Benny yelled 'Snake' and we ran to see...Cool snake! Biggest one yet."

"Yeah, crazy markings! Different from the one yesterday. Sure wish we could've caught..."

Steve interrupts Benny, "Guys, hell with the snake! This is bad. I need that knife. Help me find it. It must've flipped out and landed somewhere."

Ralph says, "Nope. Telling you I saw it just before..."

"Okay, okay, then where'd it go? It's gotta be here. Look all around the tree. Ralph you go that way and I'll take this side. Benny you look behind."

Disgusted, Benny hoots, "Behind! How would it go behind? C'mon. Waste of time."

"You gonna help or not. I'm dead if I don't put that knife back."

Benny looks suspiciously at Steve. "Thought you said it was yours?"

27

Ralph adds, "Yeah, you showed us the fleur-de-lis. The Scout thing. It was neat. We were standing right here talking and you said it was your knife!"

"Yeah, well, my dad said it will be. Just not yet." Steve kicks a rock. "I just kinda borrowed it."

Benny and Ralph laugh and point at him. Benny says, "Right. You're just kinda gonna get it for sure."

"Okay. You guys got your own knives. My dad thinks I'm too young. Twelve, too young, dumb. I need help. Are you gonna help me or not?"

Benny relents. "Okay okay, you're right, it's gotta be here. Let's do this like Hawaii Five-O. We're cops searching a field, section by section. It has to be here somewhere." He crawls around behind the tree.

"Great idea." Steve crouches down on one side and Ralph takes the other.

The three friends crawl around and finally admit defeat. Steve looks at his buddies and sighs. "Guess I gotta go home and fess up."

"Sorry Steve." Benny punches his shoulder.

Ralph yells after a retreating Steve. "Yeah, me too buddy...It'll be okay."

Steve nods and walks slowly away to face his father.

Kathe puts the potato peeler down and pushes her hair back into her head band. She adjusts her belt. She goes back to peeling potatoes and looks up as Richard closes the garage door. The setting sun highlights his still blonde hair. Kathe muses, *He looks the same as our wedding day. He's still slim...doesn't look his age...while I just keep getting older.* She sighs and puts a smile on her face to greet him.

"Hi Honey, good day?" she asks.

28

"Not bad at all. And yours?"

"Pretty good. The guy was able to fix the dryer so that's good news. We've been asked over to Aunt Bertha's for dinner on Sunday. And you should find out what's bothering Steve."

"Really? Something happen at school?"

"Don't know. He won't talk, just sits in the living room watching TV. He dragged himself in about a half hour ago, like he'd lost his best friend."

"Okay. Need a hand with dinner?" Kathe shakes her head. "Alright, I'll go see what's going on."

"Hey Buddy. What ya watching?"

"Nothing."

"Nothing? Really? Looks like something to me."

Steve stares at the TV.

"Everything okay, son?"

"Sure." Steve nervously traces his finger along the pattern in the carpet.

Richard sits beside him on the floor and tries again. "You know sometimes it helps to share a problem."

Steve squirms and stares at the TV.

"Anything wrong at school?"

Steve shakes his head.

"Trouble with your friends?"

Steve shakes his head.

"I see you don't want to talk right now, so better wash up for dinner. You know I'm there for you son." He stands and starts walking down the hall.

Steve turns. "Dad?"

Richard stops in the doorway. "Yeah Buddy?"

29

"I kinda gotta tell you something. You're going to be mad at me."

Richard sighs and walks back into the living room and sits down on the couch. "Okay, what's up?"

"Don't be mad. I didn't think I'd lose it. I had it right with me all the time. No way I could lose it. I'm so sorry. Really sorry. Don't be mad at me please."

He's terrified! What the hell did he lose this time?
"Steven. You can't have lost another thing. The list is getting too long. Your catcher's mitt, your new gym shoes. Don't get me going on those shoes, they cost an arm and a leg. And how do you lose your lunch every other day. God, what now? We had a talk. You promised to be more careful. This is getting ridiculous. What have you lost now?"

Tears fill Steve's eyes and he mumbles, "Please don't be mad at me. I took it. Ralph and Benny have one and it's so cool. They were gonna play knives after school. I wanted to play too."

"Knives? What knife?"

"I took your Boy Scout knife. You said it would be mine. I just was gonna borrow it and put it right back. Honest. We had a lot of fun. It was right there and then I don't know how it wasn't. We just went to look at the snake. It was only a second. Maybe a minute. I don't know. I'm sorry. It's gone. It vanished."

"You took my knife?...Without permission?" Richard stands up and points his finger at Steve. "This is getting way out of control young man. What in the world are we going to do with you?" He clamps his mouth shut hard. *Stop talking now. Don't lose it.* "Go to your room. I'm going to talk to your mother about this."

Steve looks up through his tears. "Dad I'm..."

30

"Go to your room, now!"

Richard sighs heavily and heads to the kitchen.

Alex walks towards his foster home happily. His hand slips into his pocket and his thumb caresses the fleur-de-lis in wonder. *It's a beaut. My dad's knife. I got it! Wow. That stupid Steve's in shit now.* He pulls it out, laughs to himself and stabs the air, *one, two,* faster, faster, *mine, all, mine.* He smiles and slips the Boy Scout knife back into his pocket. *I got the knife Steve and you'll get hell for losing it, serves you right you bastard.*

Robert MacDonald's car sits at the side of the street. *What the hell's my wonderful caseworker doing here now?* Alex approaches carefully and sits on the ground under Mrs Gilbert's kitchen window. He strains to hear the conversation. Tense, he picks up a hand full of pebbles and throws them into the grass, one after another. *One, two, three...*

He pictures Mrs Gilbert's mean face as she harangues Robert MacDonald, "I tell you there's something wrong with that boy." He sees her cold eyes narrowed into slits by her hair cruelly pulled into a bun. He sees her familiar crooked index finger jabbing the air. He feels Robert's pain...*eight, nine...*

She rattles on, "He's just not natural. Never talks. Just looks at me. Angry, that's what he is. Angry. He needs some pills. You tell that doctor he needs help. I don't think I can keep him much longer."

Robert sits straight and says, "We'll move him immediately then. No problem." He starts to stand...*fourteen, fifteen...*

Pleased, Mrs Gilbert asks, "Okay then. When can I get my next kid? I want a boy. An older boy. Girls are useless. I need help you know."

31

Robert shakes his head. *Not likely I'm going to place anyone else here.* "Sorry. We have no boys the right age at present. We'll be in touch."

"Well now just a minute. Let's not be hasty. I never said I wouldn't keep him. He's a good worker, just strange. Makes me uncomfortable. You just take him to that doctor today and tell him he needs a pill. Lots of strange things happening around here you know."

Robert stops. "What kind of strange things?"

Mrs Gilbert moves uneasily in her chair. "Well, I'm not saying it's the kid but I keep finding dead animals around... mice and birds and..."

Robert snorts. "For heaven's sake, cats do that all the time."

"Yeah we had a few cats around the neighbourhood. Two are missing and one turned up electrocuted. How does a cat do that?"

"Well I agree with you, that's a strange thing. But I'd be careful about what you're implying."

"Did I say that? Did I? Just said strange things happen around here. You just take that kid and get him a pill."

Robert shakes his head as he leaves. *Yeah I'll take the kid but I'll make sure he's okay.*

As Alex listens, he gets angrier and angrier. *You old bitch. All you want is the money. Do this, do that...I hate you.* Rage fills him and the last pebble flies from his hand. His breathing quickens, then slows, he slumps onto his side. The Strong farm flows into his mind, he's hiding in the hay loft...

Mr Strong's contorted face enters the barn muttering, "Where are you, you little bastard? Think you can hide from me? Show yourself or you'll be sorry." He steps

32

carefully, silently across the dirt floor. He hears a scrape overhead. "The hayloft! Gotcha now." He climbs the ladder. Alex cowers in the corner. "Hiding eh? Now you're gonna get it." He stomps menacingly towards the frightened boy. Alex looks around frantically, sees the loft door and leaps, but Strong's meaty hand grabs his arm mid-air.

Strong laughs. "Gotcha." He swings him around and drives his fist into his stomach. Alex crumples, face down, unable to breathe. Strong grabs him by the shirt collar, lifts him up and slams his fist into the side of his neck. Alex reels and collapses. "Get up you bastard. I'm not done yet."

Alex lays motionless. Strong looks at him suspiciously, prods him with his foot. "Whatta wuss! Can't take a punch." He laughs, stands over his slight, crumpled body. Alex begins to recover as Strong turns to leave. Alex sees his chance and leaps for the loft door. Strong grabs his shirt and pulls him back. "So you wanna fly. Okay, let's see you fly." He lifts him by his shirt collar and belt and throws him out the opening.

Alex lands with a sickening crack on a shovel handle, sees his arm lying at an odd angle and passes out.

Embroiled in his nightmare he doesn't hear Robert approach.

"Alex, let's go." Alex remains unresponsive. "Alex? Let's go now."

Alex starts, looks up, tries to focus. "Right, go. Okay."

Robert parks his car in the clinic lot, turns to Alex and says, "We'll find a new placement for you. Everything'll be okay."

Alex snorts, "I don't want a new placement. Old lady Gilbert's fine. I can handle this. At least she doesn't beat me. She feeds me. It's okay."

Robert searches Alex's face and nods. "Okay. But if for any reason you aren't happy you'll let me know at once. Deal?" Alex nods.

"Right now we're here to see Dr Gardener, the Children's Aid doctor, just to check that everything's all right." Alex stares off at nothing as he steps across the lot and into the building.

Alex sits on the examination table and waits as the doctor speaks to Robert standing in the doorway. "The boy's in good health, isn't malnourished, is clean, physically well looked after. But I'm concerned, he appears detached, anxious and if I'm not mistaken, deeply angry. We'll try a medication called Melton which works well on most anxiety based problems. We'll see how he responds. A psychiatrist may be next. This is not something to fool around with. Keep an eye on him and bring him back in a month."

In the car Robert explains about the medication and how important it is to take it regularly. Alex listens impassively. *Yeah right. One more way to ignore me. If you think I'm going to listen to any of you...just counting the days until I'm free of all you assholes.* Ruby laughs, ***Free, you will never be free you bastard. You useless bastard.*** *Mother, I wish you'd shut the fuck up.*

34

Chapter Six — Summer of 1963

June 1963

Alexander's eyes focus on boring wall paper. He pulls the blanket closer as he looks around his bedroom. *Whatta dump! At least it has a window. This bed is the pits. When I get my own place I'll get an amazing bed. Soft. With lots of blankets. I'll sleep 'til noon if I want.* ***You'll never have anything. Useless, you're useless.*** Alex rolls onto his back, takes a deep breath. *Shut up Mother. You're dead, remember? I watched you die, best day of my life.* ***And now I'm here forever…and you're useless.*** Alex moans and swings his feet to the floor. *One more month. I can do it.*

Alex enters the kitchen and gets a cereal box from the cupboard. He reaches for the milk carton and pours enough to cover the flakes. *Could be worse.* George Freeman's smiling face appears in his mind and he smiles to himself. *George was the best old man…Farmer Strong was evil, barely survived him! And now, Gilbert's a bitch. Next month I'm free — I get my own place.* He looks up as Mrs Gilbert enters.

She starts right in on him. "You've got your chores after school. There's the lawn and that garden has to be dug. Don't go wandering off like yesterday, you got chores."

Alex continues to eat. Between mouthfuls he says, "Yes, Mrs Gilbert, I'll be here."

"You were supposed to finish digging the garden last week. It's June already. Should've been planted a week ago. If you can't keep up you'll be moving I tell you."

"Yes Mrs Gilbert." *Next month…freedom.*

"You get off to school now. And come right home."

35

Home, yeah right, sure, this is a home. **You ruined our home, my Richard left us because of you...***Drop dead again Mom.* "Yes Mrs Gilbert." *You old hag!*

The final bell releases the horde onto the street. Alex leans on the railing, letting the chatty crowd pass by. *And there he is, Steven the Great, surrounded by girls and guys who want to be like him. God I wish he was dead...*Steven strides to the bike rack and pulls out his black Schwinn. Cynthia brushes against his side, giggles and looks into his eyes. She leans forward, showing her cleavage and then walks off. Steven smirks at two of the guys and pushes off, swinging his leg over his prized Schwinn. *I gotta wipe that smile off that ugly face.* Ruby's voice intrudes, **Yeah, you're gonna do something, yeah sure.**

Alex walks alone down the road. *All they want me to do is take my pills...and be a zombie. No, that's not for me. If I don't take my pills, then I have to listen to my mother, the Doc says she's not really there...tell her that. I think I'll stay in control and be nuts.* **You are nuts, worthless and nuts.** *Dad loves Steve more, and I get nothing.* Alex slams his fist into his other hand. *Nothing, I got nothing. There has to be something I can do...I'll...I'll wreck his bike. Yeah, he loves that thing. That'll show him.* Ruby laughs, **You, do something?...you're worthless.**

Alex brushes a fly off his knee, looks out over Lake Winnipeg. He shifts on his limestone perch at the end of the breakwater and throws rocks into the harbour mouth, one after another....the wind drops...the water smooths...and the fly lands again. Hunger gnaws. Soothed by the repetition, he counts the rocks as he heaves them...*one, two, three, four.* A

36

stomach growl interrupts the silence. *I'm so hungry.* He picks his way over the rubble and walks into town to The Lake and Steak. *Best burgers, best. Thank God for my grass cutting money.*

Alex sits alone at a picnic table facing the lake and munches absently on his burger. He gazes beyond the beach, out over the lake, his mind working on a plan. *Bikes are easy to steal, just ride off. But what then? I could put it in the lake, off the pier, yeah, off the pier. I can see it, sinking and disappearing. God, his dad'd just buy him a new one. How many could I steal? Naw, it has to be something else, it has to be wrecked so he can see it. All mangled, messed up.*

Alex watches as a figure approaches speeding down the lane. Steve stands on the pedals and drives his legs down hard. His Schwinn's a blur as it flies past. He doesn't notice the lone diner or feel his anger.

Tonight…I'm taking that bike…tonight.

Lights out. Daddy Richard and evil Kathe are in bed…and little angel Steve dreams of his bike, his beautiful Schwinn. Alexander slips between the garage and house where the bike leans casually on the garage wall. *Ya gotta love Gimli… nobody locks anything.* He wheels it carefully to the lane and pushes off, the tires humming on the concrete as he gains speed. Alex revels in the freedom as the breeze pushes against his face. *Wow this is flying. What a bike.* Ruby laughs, ***My God, you did something. It'll go wrong, you're useless.*** *Can't you just back off Mom.* As he speeds down the back lane he wonders what to do now. On the street, an idea stops Alex and he looks back. *That's it! The old man's car's in the driveway. I can jam the bike under the back wheel and presto in the*

37

morning...bye bye bike.

Back at the Oddleifson's house he looks closely at the angles. *Daddy Richard'll come out, get in his car and drive backwards. It'll work, I'm sure.* Alex jams the Schwinn under the rear tire of the car. *Great! Even a small move will buckle the frame. And he'll be blamed...this feels so good.* He checks every angle making sure the bike isn't noticeable. His mother's voice intrudes, ***It'll never work, you're useless.*** Alex sighs but ignores his mother. A big grin moves over his face as he imagines the mangled mess in the morning.

Alexander takes a drink at the school water fountain, straightens and leans back, watching the kids interacting. A voice calls out, "Gonna get a summer job, Alex?" He turns around.

"Hope so, Barry."

"You hear about Steve's bike?"

"You mean Steve Oddleifson? He got a bike?"

"Yeah, Oddleifson. Left it behind his dad's car and it's toast."

"God, that's dumb."

"Now he says he didn't do it...lame, dead lame."

Alex smiles, savouring the vision.

The Postal Clerk steps in front of Alex and Barry as they read the Help Wanted listings at the Post Office. She staples three new job postings on the board.

"Hey Barry. Here it is! Fisherman's helper. I've always liked fishing."

"The hell you do. You never go fishing. I'm the fisher guy, I spend my whole bloody summer filleting."

"What's filleting?"

"Whaa?"

"Just kidding, but you're right. I never go fishing, but that's not what I'm gonna say when I apply for this job." Alex looks around and decides to tell Barry his news.

"Barry I get my own place soon, in July."

"You're kiddin', how's that work?"

"Turn eighteen, all grown up, get my own place."

"So where's this place?"

"Have a meeting with my caseworker to get all the details...You lookin' for work too?" Alex asks.

"Nah, I gotta work for my Dad…you know, up in the bush. Fly-in camp. No girls, no fun…it sucks. Do you know where your place'll be?"

"No, that's what the meeting's about. I really don't know all the rules yet. But I'll get to choose it myself."

Barry looks at him. "Cool. Lucky bastard."

The sign reads 'Erikson's Fish'.

Nervously Alex brushes nothing off his shirt. *Hope I look good enough.*

Peter Erikson steps out of the filleting shed. Fish blood, a few streams of slime, patches of fish skin and scales adorn his worn, stiff work overalls.

Alex looks at him. *I guess I look good enough.* He offers his hand, Peter wipes his on his front and they shake.

"So, you're Alex Gislason, and you want to be a fisherman's helper."

"Yes Sir."

"You're hired."

"That was fast."

39

"A helper can do what a helper can do. If you can do enough, I'll keep you. Otherwise this might be a very short job."

"When do I start?"

"Go home and change into some old clothes and you start in an hour."

"Done."

Alex, wearing his ripped jeans and an old 'T' shirt with 'BORN to DIE' fading on the front, knocks on the door of the filleting shed. Nothing happens. *I can hear him in there.* He bangs on the door. A voice yells, "So get in here." Alex opens the door and nearly falls back, hit by the smell of old and new fish guts, dried and fresh slime, blood, scales and fish carcasses and neat piles of boxed fillets. "Grab a knife, make yourself useful."

Alex looks around, finds a knife that looks like the one Mr Erikson holds and stands beside him at the table.

"These are white fish. First cut behind the gills." He holds the fish by the tail, deftly cuts down to the spine. "Run the blade beside the backbone," the knife slides, plowing scales, "and just past the asshole," he turns the carcass and Alex sees the anus, "you slip your knife through." Jerry runs the knife past the end of the tail and the fish flexes.

It's still alive! Alex sucks in a breath. *God, This's exciting!*

Peter Erikson pulls back the flesh beside the spine. "Run your blade against the rib cage and keep pulling the fillet back." Like magic, the fillet rolls off the ribs in front of the knife. "The belly has all those fins and the butt. Cut around them." One smooth cut and the fillet is free. "Skin it." He grabs the tail end and slides his knife against the skin in one

40

motion. "This is boneless." He hands it to Alex. "Run your fingers along the fillet, check for bones."

Alex runs his fingers along the flesh and feels an urge in his groin. *I love this job.*

Peter flips the fish and completes the other fillet faster than Alex can follow. The head, guts and tail slide as a unit down the hole in the table. "Okay, Alexander, you try one now. I'm not gonna watch you for the first few, unless you ask. Give it a try."

Alex grabs a fish by the tail and pulls it over in front of him. It flexes. A thrill passes up his arm. He saws at the scales behind the gills and suddenly the knife cuts to the spine. Alex gasps. His groin tightens and a wave of energy spreads through his body. He presses his crotch against the table as he runs his blade down the backbone. It slices to the rib cage, ploughs through the scales, carves around the back fin. At the anus he drives it through. A spasm flexes Alex's gut. Pent up semen spurts into his underwear. *God! I love this.*

August 1963

Alexander deflects a branch, steps carefully through the underbrush — a flash of movement, he freezes. The rabbit freezes, listening. Alex slowly lifts his 22, squeezes. The report ripples away, echoes back. The rabbit's rear legs jerk. *Running and going nowhere.* He picks up his prize by the ears, a few final spasms convulse the corpse.

He tramps out of the bush, through the ditch and onto Highway 9. It's a short walk to his new place on Sixth Avenue. He drops the rabbit at the back door and heads down the basement stairs to his Studio Apartment. *Fancy.* He laughs. *Stoodio Apartment. But what the heck, it's all mine.*

41

He looks around at his unmade bed and the sink filled with dirty dishes. *Yeah all mine. No one can tell me to do anything. Gotta get my knife.* He reaches under the bed and pulls out his cigar box. *My treasures.* He opens the lid, picks up the blue ear ring, rolls it around in his palm and pictures his mother choking. He chuckles to himself, then looks at the two decks of cards, sighs. He grabs the Boy Scout knife and heads outside to the rabbit.

He pedals out South Colonization Road with the rabbit's body draped over the handle bar. He turns at McCurdy's equipment shed. *My quiet island, yes, my Angel Sigga, I come to be with you.* He settles into his spot between the shed and the derelict tractor, lays down the rabbit and leans back. *My Angel, blue dress, sparkling blue, light from you, sparkling blue.* He shifts onto his side, lying down in the grass. *Death to you Steve…Yeah, death. You can hold her hand, but she's mine, mine.* With the knife in his right hand he sits and takes hold of the rabbit. *Death to you Steve…with your own knife…* he pushes the point into the rabbit's gut. It resists, then suddenly slips inside. Alex gasps. He works the blade upwards, cutting the belly wide open. He pulls the fur back and looks into the cut. *Can't see much.* He makes a cross-cut under the ribs and again across the lower belly from leg to leg. He pulls back the flaps. *Now that's guts.* Then the smell hits him.

He shudders and uses the blade to dig a hole next to the shed. He pulls the warm, stinking innards free of the rabbit and drops them in. He cuts the strings of slime and sinew and looks at the gutted corpse. He scrapes out the remaining pieces of the rabbit's guts and buries them with the mess in the hole.

Alex sits it against the tractor tire and leans back to admire his creation. It slumps to the side. He takes a stick and props it up. It falls the other way. He jams two sticks into the fur on the back of the paws and leans them against the tire at a sharp angle. They hold the rabbit upright. *That'll hold Mr Steve Rabbit. Now that's gorgeous. So, Steve, how do you feel now?* **You really are crazy. That's not Steve. You're a loser.** *I don't care what you think Mother, you're dead. I just killed Steve so Angel Sigga's mine, not his, mine, all mine.*

Alexander gathers a handful of sticks, stokes a small fire and leans back, satisfied, enjoying the late afternoon sun on his face. *It doesn't get much better than this.* The flames dance and he sees the form of his Angel in the flames. *Sigga, my Angel, I love you. Sparkling blue, I love you. We'll live in a big house by the lake, have a deck and go swimming every day. I love you.*

43

Chapter Seven — Alexander Confronts Richard

July 1966

Alexander bursts out of the lawyer's office. Stunned, he thinks, *What the hell? Twenty thousand dollars? I've got twenty thousand dollars! Where would my stupid mother get that kind of money?* He shakes his head, paces on the street in front of the office.

Robert MacDonald calmly closes the office door and approaches Alexander. "Okay, are we clear here? You understood what the lawyer said?"

Alexander looks at him. "No. What the hell? Twenty thousand dollars?"

Robert sighs. "Yes, it's the money that was put in trust for you when your mother died. I can't tell you what to do with it, but as your social worker and I hope your friend, I suggest you either invest it or maybe buy a house. Don't blow it. It's unlikely you'll ever see a lump sum like this again."

"Christ! Twenty thousand dollars! There's no way."

Robert smiles and puts his hand on Alexander's shoulder. "What's to understand? Your mother obviously had money in her estate and now it's yours."

Alex shakes off Robert's hand, "Right. My mother. Yeah, sure." *Idiot, my mother didn't have a pot to piss in. She drank every nickel she got her hands on. Where'd this money come from?*

Robert talks slowly, "Alex, this is a great windfall for you. I hope you use the money wisely. This is important."

44

Alex looks at him and smirks. "Yeah, wisely." He looks over at his third or fourth hand truck. *I'll use it wisely all right. New truck here I come.*

Robert watches him eye his truck. "A new truck is definitely not a good investment…"

Alex interrupts him, "I got a great gig with this old fisherman. I look after him, help him do a little fishing and he lets me live in his place. Got no bills, man. A new truck is exactly what I need."

Robert shakes his head. "Alex, listen…"

Alex continues to pace. An idea is taking shape when Robert's voice intrudes, "Alex please listen to…"

Alex stops. "No, you listen. I'm twenty-one now. I don't have to listen to anyone anymore." He looks pointedly at Robert, then turns away. *God! There's only one place that much money could've come from.* And he walks off.

Robert calls after him, "Hey, you forgot your truck."

"S'okay, need to walk."

Robert sighs*, always weird,* climbs into his own vehicle and drives off.

Alexander storms down Third Avenue. *Son of a bitch! It's gotta be that fucking father of mine! Jesus. Ignores me my whole life and now I get the big payoff. God damned Richard Oddleifson…never a nickel and now the big pay off! Everything for Steve, nothing for me…Ruins my life and now 'Everything's OK!' Sure, buy me off! Well we'll just see about that. Too little, too late.*

Alexander reaches the north government ditch and turns towards the lake. He clambers down onto the sand, turns and walks back towards town. *Asshole thinks he can buy me off.* He punches his fist into the air. *There isn't enough money in the world to buy me off, not even a million, you son of a bitch.*

45

Alexander stands still. *Well, maybe all of his money might be enough. Yeah! All his God damn money...that'd do it. Leave him with nothing. The son of a bitch. Yeah and that little bastard Steve! No expensive bikes and shoes and...Right... leave the buggers with nothing. That feels good...* Alexander looks out over the lake, stands still and yells, "All you sons of bitches should have nothing...Nothing!"

He runs down the beach towards town, stops behind the Oddleifson house, sits down on the sand and watches the garage...*Jesus, twenty thousand dollars! Buy me off? I'm going to shove it down his throat. That's what I'm gonna do. Shove it down his throat. Maybe he'll choke on it. Yeah, choke! Choke and die. Down his throat. I'll watch him choke. He'll be broke. The son of a bitch. Watching him choke... good. Sputtering and choking and I just stand there and...*

The garage door opens, interrupting Alexander's chaotic thoughts. He watches Richard's Grand Marquis crawl slowly towards the garage. He runs across the lane and enters just behind the car. Richard steps out and Alex yells, "You son of a bitch!"

Startled, Richard turns around. "Excuse me? Can I help you?"

"Help me?" Alex laughs. "Help me? It's a little too late."

Richard takes off his sunglasses. "Now just a minute,"... *What the...he's furious!...* "Who are you? What're you talking about?"

"Don't you know me, Daddy? Don't I look familiar? How could I? You abandoned me, you prick."

Richard's face pales as he takes a step forward. "Alexander?" *My God!*

"Yeah, it's me."

46

"My God, what're you doing here?" *This can't be happening.* "There is nothing here for you. You shouldn't be here."

Alexander snorts. "Oh yeah, I know that. Nothing for me. Everything for Steve."

"There's no point in any of this. You should leave. I have nothing to say. I'm sorry you're upset, but it's ancient history now. Please go."

"I'll go when I'm damn good and ready. I came here to tell you to stuff the twenty thousand dollars up your ass."

"Twenty thousand dollars?"

"Yeah, your blood money. Just got it from the lawyers. I'm twenty-one now, I'm an adult. You ignore me for years, and now you think money can make up for my miserable life?"

Alex steps nearer, Richard steps back, says, "I know nothing about any money. I want you to leave. Go!"

"Go?" Alex laughs menacingly. "Go? Not yet. Not before I ram it down your miserable throat."

"Now you listen here…"

"No, you listen. You're finally gonna listen. You left me in hell, old man. Hell! You hear me?" Alexander steps towards him, finger jabbing. "Wanna know the life you gave me? Foster families…foster…fucking…families. You know what that's like. Beatings, broken bones, starving, no love." Alex snorts. "Love…right, what's that? You abandoned me in hell."

Close enough to touch, Alex looks steadily, firmly into Richard's eyes as his hand, almost unconsciously, wraps around the Boy Scout knife in his pocket. Their faces edge closer. Richard's mind reels. *What the hell's going on? He's trouble! Real trouble.* Richard turns towards the door. "I'm calling the police."

47

Alex freezes, catatonic. *I need a hug, Joe, hug me, be my friend.* He looks at his father's back, starts crying, and in a very small voice says, "Why couldn't you love me? I was just a little boy. I loved you...no one's ever loved me."

Richard hesitates, his hand on the door knob, his head sags and his shoulders slowly droop, but he doesn't turn around. *So much pain...God forgive me.* "It's too late, Alexander. Too much time has passed. We have to move on." He turns around and faces him, says, "I'm sorry. Go now before..."

Alexander's rage explodes and his right hand flashes out.

The Boy Scout knife slashes deep below Richard's left ear. His eyes bulge, he grabs his neck, blood spurts between his fingers. Alex pulls the knife back and pushes it weakly several times against his chest as Richard drops. "Thanks for everything, Daddy, you son of a bitch."

Richard falls at his feet. Alex stands over him, breathing hard, his rage slowly abates. *Christ, that's a lot of blood.* He breathes deeply, smiles, steps back and leans one hip on the car. *So you wouldn't marry my mother, you S O B.* He reaches down and wipes the blade on his father's sleeve, looks at him for a moment, then pulls off his wedding ring. "This is for my miserable excuse of a mother...Mother? Nothing to say? Finally quiet?" He chuckles to himself.

Still laughing, Alexander looks out the raised garage door. Seeing no one, he steps out and walks casually down the back lane.

Chapter Eight — Alexander Sees his Angel

Thirty-nine years later
December 2005

Alexander rolls and groans. Oh God…my head! He opens one eye and focuses on the blurry clock. *7:30, God…how much did I drink?* He moves his head slightly, winces and shifts his eye over to the window, the broken venetian blind obscures his view of swirling snow. *God, snowing again. Will it ever stop?* He opens his other eye. His legs swing to the floor and hit an empty soup bowl. Kicking it out of the way, he stands, scratches his genitals and heads to the toilet.

He relieves himself, then leans against the rusty sink and holds his face under the cold water. He lifts his head to look in the streaked mirror and water runs down his unkempt beard. He looks closely at his face. A memory flickers and he grimaces, *Merry bloody Christmas! Thank God that's over for another year.* He examines his face critically. *I look like I'm eighty, not sixty.* He groans and puts his face under the icy water until it hurts. *I need a drink.*

He walks carefully into the kitchen trying not to jar his pounding head. A quart of sour milk has spilled on the table and oozed onto the floor, joining an unidentifiable puddle in front of a pile of laundry. The putrid odours hit him. He gags, clutches his mouth and runs back into the bathroom. His body arches in rhythm with the retching, his head pounds… exhausted, he sits back on the floor and moans. *Great. Dry heaves.* His stomach churns. He leans over the bowl and tries to vomit again. He leans against the tub waiting for the nausea to pass. *Look at me. I'm an idiot.* ***You're an idiot. Look at***

49

yourself. Puking your guts up. Drinking by yourself. Idiot. Loser. "Shut up Mother. I don't need you, I need a drink."

He pulls himself up using the sink, stumbles back into the kitchen, opens the fridge door and looks at the emptiness. *No beer. Now I'm screwed. Maybe there's some rotgut left. Hahahaha, yeah sure, right!* Without real hope he looks under the sink, nothing. Opens the cupboard over the fridge, smiling he reaches for a small bottle near the back. He reads, 'Electric Oil.' He opens the cap and recoils at the odour. *Geez, must be old Harry's. Wonder what he used it for? He sure was a great old guy. Gave me all of this didn't he?* Alex looks around and smiles. Pulling himself back to reality he mumbles, "If I don't get a drink, today'll be hell...where?" He burps loudly and winces at the sour taste as he looks through the junk on the couch, then heads to the bedroom.

He tears off the blanket and sheet. Nothing. *For Christ sake.* He slumps down on the mattress, grabs his pounding head with both hands and leans on his knees. His fingers slide through greasy hair. *Ugh. Need a shower, but first booze. Where are my God damn pants?* He opens his eyes and spies a pant leg sticking out from under the bed. *Bingo!* He fumbles in his pockets...nothing. *Money. I need money.* A sobering thought penetrates the fog. *What day is it anyway? Hope it's not Boxing Day...nothing open on bloody Boxing Day.* He stands and looks at the wall calendar. *Twenty seventh! Thank God. Now money. There's gotta be money somewhere in this mess, I know I cashed my pogey.* He rips into his dresser drawers, finds several crumpled twenty dollar bills. *Jackpot! May as well take the empties to the Oldie and then treat myself to some rye at the LC.*

Alexander pulls into the liquor store parking lot and leans

50

back to ease his headache. *Why the hell can't the LC open at nine like everyone else? Six more minutes. I'll just close my eyes.*

An hour later he's awakened by laughter and sits up, disoriented. Two men are talking close to his truck. *God, must've passed out.*

In the whiskey aisle he locates the cheapest bottle and heads to the check-out. There's a woman ahead of him talking to the cashier. Eyes down, he puts his weight on one foot and then the other, his need for booze grinds inside him. *Hurry the fuck up lady.* He closes his eyes and listens to the conversation. The lady in the blue coat is asking about Beaujolais. Alexander snorts. *Another privileged asshole. Beaujolais my ass.* The woman gestures with her arm and a scent floats past his face. Alexander breathes deeply. *Apples. I smell apples.* He opens his eyes and looks closely at the woman in front of him. Her blonde hair brushes the collar of her blue coat and a memory of another time pushes through the mental fog. He moves closer and hears her saying, "That's very kind of you. I would appreciate a call when they arrive. Can I leave you my number?"

Her voice sounds like music. Like a song. His mind fills with the image of a girl in a light blue dress, the sun backlighting her blonde hair, giving her a halo…like an angel. He feels an urge in his groin. *My Angel.* He shakes his head. *Don't be an ass. No fool like an old fool. Right?*

The cashier asks for her name and number.

"Sigga Johnson, 642-7…" Alexander's eyes snap wide. *Sigga, my Angel Sigga. It's you. Oh my God!* He moves closer to see her face. Sigga catches a whiff of something unpleasant and steps back. Alexander moves away and mumbles, "Sorry." He looks at his reflection in the window behind the

51

cashier. *Look at me. I'm a mess. I stink! God, I stink. I'd scare children. My Angel Sigga, right in front of me. And look at me. She's disgusted. I'm a drunk, a bum.* He feels like crying. He wants to yell, *'This isn't me. It isn't me'.* Tears well up as Sigga turns to leave. He dumps his money on the counter and runs out after her. Dumbstruck, the cashier calls after him… "Mister, your change." He shakes his head.

Outside, he jumps in his truck and follows Sigga's car. She turns onto Third Avenue and makes another turn further down. She heads into the back lane. He stops and watches her park in back of the old Oddleifson house. *Is she visiting?* She takes out her house keys and lets herself into the house. *Lives here! My Angel Sigga is back!*

Alexander sits quietly as joy fills his chest and works its way up to his face. His smile is so foreign he touches it in wonder. *What the hell? My Sigga, here in Gimli. I have a chance. A chance!* He puts the truck in gear and checks himself in the rear view. His smile disappears as quickly as it came. *Look at me! Who would ever want me?*

A nasty chuckle echoes inside his head. ***You got that right. Who would ever want you? No one, that's who. Look at yourself. You're a bum. A stinking, drunken bum.***

Alexander beats on the steering wheel, yells, "Shut up Mother. I'm all grown up. I'm sixty now, you can leave. I'm a good boy. But someone has to love me. Someone has to…" He lays his head on the steering wheel and his body shakes as his cries turn to gasping sobs. Finally still, he sits quietly resting his head on his arms, repeating over and over, "I'm a good boy. Sigga will love me."

He looks at himself again in the rear view mirror. *I'll change. I'll quit drinking. I'll clean up. I can do it.* He looks longingly at the whiskey bottle in the brown bag. His body aches. *I'll sober up…First I need a drink.*

Chapter Nine — Alexander Gets Clean

January 2006

Alexander's feet sink in beach sand not yet warmed by the sun. A flock of seagulls squawk, "Danger! Danger!" He watches their frightened flight and smiles. *Silly birds. I'm no danger to you.* The sun breaks the horizon, leisurely rising, flooding the lake with morning light. Warmth invades his chest, spreads and lights up his face. *Peace. Is this what I feel? Peace?* Words push their way around his brain, working together, making sounds, images, rhyming, repeating. *Yes, I used to write poetry...can I put this moment into words? Poetry?* He laughs out loud, but the urge is strong and the words keep dancing. How to capture his feelings...the morning, the sun...in a poem?

New morning bright with gentle breeze,
Brings you to mind my perfect love,
My Angel Sigga full of light,
Like the sun this morn, you give me life,
You own my heart and all that is, shall be or ever was.

Maybe, not quite right.

The sun casts a handful of diamonds across the water and a band of brilliance dances to the shore at Alexander's feet. He lifts one foot and dips a toe...movement startles him. Someone approaches along the shore. *Damn, go away. This is my time. You're not wanted.* He turns to walk off but hesitates, looks closely at the figure walking towards him...*it's a*

54

woman…in a blue dress. His heart beats a little faster. *Could it be?…no…maybe.* The woman stoops to pick up something and her blonde hair shifts forward. *Oh my God. It's Sigga. It's my Angel Sigga.* His feet won't move…she gets closer and closer. He can see her face. She smiles and reaches for him. His feet are frozen in place, Alexander extends his hand. He struggles but his feet refuse to budge. *Move, damn it.* Her mouth moves but he can't make out the words. She steps close enough for their hands to touch. He stretches towards her extended fingers…

"Noooooooo." Alexander sits up in bed and screams, "Noooooooo." Tears well up and hollowness fills his chest. *Damn, a dream, just a dream.* He lies back and looks at the ceiling, breathes evenly in and out. *My Angel was right there. I almost touched her.* Through the broken blind he sees the snow swirling. He snorts. *Yeah right, walking on the beach, what a doofus…At least it beats the nightmares, and those damn sweats.* He feels his sheets and smiles. *Dry. Thank God.*

What day is it? Thursday? Friday? He mentally counts down the days. *Ten, maybe eleven days since my last drink. Wow. Have I turned a corner here?* He pans the room, afraid his mother Ruby still sits in the corner. *Thank God she's gone. Hope she's gone. Can't take another day of her screaming.* He shivers and remembers her face, skin peeling off her cheeks, patches of red hair still clinging to her scalp. *God if that didn't drive me to drink I don't know what would. Bitch! Hearing her voice's bad enough, but seeing her rotting corpse…*

I'm hungry. When was the last time I was hungry? Wonder if I have any food? He sits on the side of his bed waiting for the dizziness to start. *Nothing. Wow! Great.* He carefully stands and heads for the bathroom.

55

In the kitchen he munches a piece of toast and looks around the room. *Where to start? It's all bad...I could start anywhere. I guess the kitchen.* He searches for some cleaning supplies. *Who am I kidding? Cleaning supplies! I'll get dressed, get some food and some...what? Dutch Cleanser? Wonder if they still make that. Maybe some Windex? Or Vinegar. Whatever's cheap.*

He shades his eyes from the blinding sun and hurries to his truck. *I'll make a little detour, maybe I'll see my Angel Sigga.* He turns down Third Avenue and stops just before Sigga's house. *Everything's quiet and peaceful.* The snow on the sidewalk is undisturbed. He sits for a while hoping to get a glimpse of her. Finally, disappointed, he puts the truck in gear. *Better get going. I'll come back after the store.*

Alexander is strangely comforted by the grocery bags nestled beside him as he turns the truck down the back lane behind Sigga's. He turns off the engine and waits. *One little look. That's all I need. Come out Sigga. Come out.* Ten long, silent minutes pass, then as he reaches for the ignition keys the back door opens. A bundled up Sigga emerges with a shovel. *She's going to shovel the walk! Great.* He watches her push and throw the snow to one side. *I could offer to help.* He shakes his head. *Not yet. I'd just scare her. Better to follow my plan. Clean myself up. Clean my life up. I've got time.*

By the end of the week Alexander has cleaned the kitchen, the living area, the bedroom and scrubbed the bathroom until it almost shone. *God, look at all this clean.* He laughs and looks into the bathroom mirror. He holds his chin and examines it from different angles. *That's new! Skin looks better, really good around my beard. No booze and decent food...I'm a new*

56

man. *Time for a shave. I have a razor around here somewhere.* He laughs. *Better find scissors first.* For an hour he cuts, lathers and shaves, cuts, lathers and shaves and his skin appears. He looks at the white pallor and grimaces. *I look like a dead man. Better get some sun. Right, some sun. I wonder when the damn sun'll come out?*

Satisfied with his effort he looks around the bathroom. *Paint, what colour? What would Sigga like? I could look in her windows and see. Yeah, good idea. And do some laundry. I'll check when the laundromat isn't busy. Yes, that's a plan. I'll reconnoitre. Reconnoitre. I wonder if anything rhymes with reconnoitre? Goitre, loiter...now that'd make a fancy poem?* He laughs. *Great word, Alex. Reconnoitre...Sigga's place, paint, laundromat.*

Alexander looks at his watch. *Two o'clock and the laundromat's deserted. Okay, I'll be back tomorrow. Now let's check out Sigga's place.* He drives down the back lane and, seeing no car in the driveway, sits for a minute wondering how to approach the house. He looks at an empty box on the floor. *I could be delivering something. Now just walk up natural like. It could be fish...yup, I'm delivering fish.*

He walks nonchalantly, climbs the stairs, knocks on the back door and waits. *Great, no one home and a window right here. It'd be normal to look in for a second, right?* Shading his eyes he looks into the living room. *Pretty. Just like Sigga. All white and clean and...pretty. The couch is definitely white but what would you call the walls? Off white? No, too creamy, like butter but not yellow.* He peers in for another moment. *Look at all the books. Books everywhere. A pile on the table and a couple on the coffee table. She reads. A lot. When was the last time I read anything?*

A loud voice startles him. "What're you doin'?"

Alexander jumps and turns around to see a woman scowling at him.

"What're you doin'?" she repeats even louder.

He clears his throat, "Delivering."

"Okay, I can take it. I'm her neighbour." She gestures to the house behind her.

"No."

"No? Give it to me and I'll get it to her." The woman holds up her hands for the box and steps closer.

Alexander steps down the stairs. "No. Need to give it to her myself." He moves quickly to his truck. The woman is still standing there watching. *Bitch, mind your own business.* He speeds down the back lane. *God, close call, my heart's banging like a hammer. I need a drink. Damn.*

He hits the brake at the stop sign and looks north towards the liquor commission and then west towards KC Enterprises. *Shit, booze or paint? Booze or paint?* He shuts his eyes and leans his head on the steering wheel. Ruby starts screaming. ***You idiot. What do you think you're doing. Once a loser always a loser.*** He lifts his head and hits the pedal. *Shut up mother. Okay, get paint while I still remember the colour. Booze after. Maybe, I'll decide later.*

Wet paint brush in one hand, Alexander surveys the living area. *Nice. That looks fresh. And white.* He laughs to himself. *White, cream, off white, ridiculous. But it sure brightens the place up.* He yawns. *God, I'm exhausted. I'll think about booze tomorrow, right now, a sandwich and bed.*

A seagull startles him as he steps onto the beach. The birds take off en masse and he turns his back to avoid any poop

58

spatter as they wheel out over the lake. Half the sun is above the horizon. He walks to the water and dips one toe, then looks to his right hoping to catch sight of someone. His chest tightens as a woman comes into view. *There she is, my Sigga.* He tries to call out but his mouth makes no sound. He waits patiently for her to get closer. She nears, but hesitates and looks beyond him. Delighted, she runs past with her arms spread wide. Alexander tries to turn to see who it is, but…

"Noooo. Stop. See me! See me!" He opens his eyes. "No, see me." He whispers. He wipes his eyes with the sheet and tries to remember what happened. *Christ. There was someone else there. She was so happy to see someone else. Who was it?* He thinks about what happened, then sits up suddenly and says, "It was a lousy dream, asshole. Just a dream."

Alexander washes, paints and cleans but he can't get rid of a foreboding feeling. Every day he drives to Sigga's to watch, but sees her only once.

Wednesday, on his way to the laundromat he stops in his usual spot just down from Sigga's. Light snow settles, covers the street in white. A pedestrian walks briskly towards him, then turns onto Sigga's sidewalk! *Who's that? He looks familiar. No hat, that walk, looks a bit older than my Angel… whose walk is that?* He rolls down the window to look closer…*No, it can't be!* The man knocks on Sigga's door and it opens quickly, like she'd been standing there waiting. The door closes behind him.

Stunned, Alex tries to make sense of what he has just seen. *What the fuck? It can't be. He doesn't live here anymore. Not for years and years. Fucking Steve Oddleifson.* He bangs the steering wheel. Ruby starts chanting and laughing, ***What a***

59

loser. What a loser. You'll never be as good as Steve. Alex holds his ears and yells, "We'll just see about that."

Chapter Ten — Alexander Falls into the Bottle

February 2006

Alex slams the back door, rattling the windows. He looks around for something to throw. Ruby's voice screams, **Whatta loser. Loser Loser Loser. You're not good enough.** His neck tightens, he grimaces. *Shut up Mother…fucking Steve Oddleifson. Now think. Think. They're cousins, right? Right. Cousins. It was just…he dropped in.* He sits down and shakes his head. *Yeah, cousins. Cousins talk. It's nothing. Yeah, but fucking Steve Oddleifson…what's he doing back here? Probably visiting. Yeah, visiting. He can visit all he wants. Nothing to worry about. Shit, glad I didn't get some booze. Overreacting or what? Continue my plan. Clean up my life. Everything'll be good. Time to paint the bedroom.*

The afternoon light fades as Alexander arranges his new set of dishes on the table against the wall. *They look nice, flowers, women like flowers. Best I could get at the Basic Needs store. Cheap but pretty.* He pulls the table cloth to even it up. He imagines Sigga sitting there. *So beautiful. Yeah, I'll ask her over for lunch…someday soon, I hope.* He looks around the kitchen area, scans his living room. *Getting good… clean, neat, fresh paint…yeah, good.* He looks at the clock. *7:00, Maybe there's still time to catch sight of my Angel.*

Alex slips on his parka and heads for his truck. He fish tails a bit leaving South Beach. *God it's slippery.* He easily straightens the truck and heads to his regular spot, a half block from Sigga's. He settles back and hopes he can catch a glimpse of her. Suddenly he sits up, *What the…?*

Steve pulls up and Sigga walks carefully out and gets in his car. *What the hell?* They drive off and Alex follows them to the Lakeview Hotel. *Shit. Taking her to his room…this can't*

61

be good. He parks his truck and follows them in. *Heading for the restaurant, good...*but they turn into a banquet room. Alexander waits a minute, then steps close enough to read the sign. *Rotary Club. Jeez it's a damn Rotary meeting. What the hell's going on? What now?* He turns and leaves. *Wonder how long a meeting lasts? Maybe I'll just wait at her place and see what happens.*

Hours later, the dark envelopes a very cold and uncomfortable Alex. Discouraged, he reaches towards the ignition when a car pulls up. Steve gets out and escorts Sigga to her door. Alex slouches down and watches intently. They laugh and slide on the icy sidewalk. At the front steps Sigga slips and starts to go down. Steve catches her and they're face to face. Steve leans down, their lips touch, Sigga moves closer. *Shit! They're kissing. Kissing! That's a kiss. Not a cousinly kiss. That's a fucking kiss! What the hell?* He sits up and peers into the darkness. Steve and Sigga talk for a moment and then say goodbye at the door. *Cousins don't kiss. What's going on? Why're you still here Steven, you bastard? You don't belong here. I'm gonna follow you.* Alex keeps a respectable distance on the deserted roads. Steve drives past the hotel and heads north. *What the hell?* Steve turns into Loni Beach and down Lake Avenue. A garage door opens and Steve drives inside. *Christ. He fucking lives here.* Alexander looks at the upscale house with its big timbers and lake rock exterior. *Of course only the best for fucking Oddleifson. I've been a fool. A damn fool.*

He floors the pedal, fishtails down the street, screaming, "Fucking Steve Oddleifson. Gets everything." Ruby laughs insanely. ***Told you. Told you. You're a loser. Biggest loser. You lose everything.*** "Shut up Mother, leave me alone."

62

He picks up speed on the highway and barely makes the turn into the Viking beer vendor. Screaming at Ruby, he slams on the brake, his truck slides to an angled stop. The driver in the next car locks his door. Alexander gives him the finger and runs into the vendor.

"A two four."

The startled clerk asks, "Of?"

"Shit, don't care."

The clerk grabs the first case in the cooler and pushes it toward Alexander.

He slams down his money and runs out the door.

The clerk stammers, "Hey, your change?"

At home he plunks the two four on the table and rips it open. He guzzles one bottle, a second and a third. Ruby screams, *What a loser. You can't do nothing right. You'll never be as good as Steve.*

He grabs his head and falls to his knees. "Bitch…leave me alone. Leave me alone." He cries, curls up in a fetal position and lies still, sobbing. His voice gets quieter, "Leave me alone, leave…"

Alex opens his eyes and quickly closes them. The sun is streaming relentlessly through his clean windows. *What the hell? What am I doing on the couch?* He sits up slowly and scans the room, beer bottles, some broken, litter the floor. The image of Steve and Sigga kissing forms. "Noooo. Not my Sigga, my Angel Sigga. That bastard Steve!"

He struggles to his feet and kicks the empty beer box across the room…*You're not good enough*…*Fuck you Mother*…Rage courses through his body and he looks at the dishes and screams. "Bastard, you fucking bastard." He grabs

63

the table cloth and pulls, dishes crash to the floor. He picks up pieces that survived and throws them one by one at the freshly painted wall. Still not satisfied, he picks up a kitchen chair and beats the wall over and over, the wood splinters, one leg penetrates the drywall. He pulls on the chair but it's lodged tightly. "Shit!" He pulls back and drives his fist into the wall. White hot pain shoots up to his shoulder and stops him. He looks in wonder at his screaming hand. Rage consumes him, almost blocking out Ruby...*Loser, loser, loser*...Wildly he looks around the room. "Not enough."

Ruby screams, *What an idiot! Look at what you've done. Complete loser!* He kicks open the outside door, blinks at the brightness. *What to smash? I'd smash you Mother if I could get my hands on you.* Ruby laughs, *Idiot! Loser! You'll never win...never!* Ignoring the cold, he scans the yard. A flash of orange catches his attention. *Cat!* He modulates his voice, "Hey kitty kitty kitty. Pretty kitty." The cat peers from behind his truck tire but doesn't move. *Need something...It looks hungry.* He returns with a piece of bologna. "Here kitty gotta nice piece of meat here." The animal takes a cautious step. "That's a good kitty. C'mon now. Nice meat." Alexander waves it slowly back and forth. It's too much for the starving cat. Abandoning caution it snaps at the meat. With his good hand he scoops it up. He watches as the cat devours the meat and talks quietly to the starving animal. Meat finished, the cat squirms and tries to escape but Alexander grabs it around the neck and twists sharply. His hand protests and he cries out. The cat is still. Alexander smiles. Ruby is quiet.

He sits holding the dead cat, looking off into space. *Who was I kidding? I am a loser. I'll never have anything. Steve gets it all. All the time. Everything I want he gets. When will it stop?* Tears trickle down his lined face. The crying turns into

64

sobs and his whole body shakes. Finally the sobbing subsides and he shivers. *Christ I'm cold. Cold and useless. Useless. Mother's right.* Ruby cackles, ***Ha ha I'm right. Useless, useless, useless.***

Alex stands, shoulders slumped and turns into the house, "Leave me alone Mother." He looks around at the carnage, "What's the use of anything. I am a loser, will always be a loser." He goes into the bedroom, climbs into the new coloured sheets, pulls the blankets over his face and silently weeps.

Chapter Eleven — Alexander Loses It

March 2006

Alex opens the last cupboard door, slams it, sneers and says out loud, "Not one clean cup." He looks at the overflowing sink and sighs. "Coffee. I need coffee but beer'll always do." Who wants to sober up anyway. *What's it been? Weeks? Who cares?* "I've got nothing now." He peers into his empty fridge. "Shit!" *There has to be a beer somewhere.* He looks at the empty beer bottles littered everywhere. He pleads, "Just one. Need one." He picks up a beer case and shakes it...nothing. He kicks one, it flies, hits the wall and lands on top of another box. He grabs that one hopefully. "Empty." He sighs, sits down on the lone kitchen chair and looks out into the darkness. "Guess I'll have to make a beer run."

Alex looks longingly at the case of beer on his front seat. "Nearly home. Hang on." The back lane on Fourth Avenue is dark and he drives carefully. "Gotta stay off the main roads, never know where the bloody fuzz are and wouldn't they just love to catch me again." He laughs quietly to himself. A burst of light startles him, he slams on the brakes. BOOM! A thundering roar rumbles across Gimli. He turns his head towards the light and gapes as a crimson dome rises above Third Avenue. "Shit!" *That looks like it's close to my Ang...no not, not my Angel.* His eyes fill with tears. Sirens scream closer and closer. "I better get home. Too drunk for cops." *But what if it's her house?* More sirens join the others until the whole night is alive with noise and light. "Sheeit!" *I gotta go take a look. They gotta be too busy to bother with me.*

66

He creeps slowly down Third Avenue, gapes at the glowing red smoke-filled sight, cop cars, fire trucks, silhouettes of people running. And Sigga's house engulfed in flames, backlighting the whole area. *Oh no! It can't be. Not my Angel. No way she survives this.* Stunned, he stops, watching but not seeing anything in his anguish. *She's dead...my Angel's dead.* Suddenly a cop bangs on his window. "Move on. Nothing here to see. Move on."

Alex nods, hits the gas and speeds off. Tears now blind him as he picks up speed, faster and faster, hurtling down Third Avenue, roaring through stop signs until he is at the government ditch. He screams past the Senior Centre as his speedometer hits 130kph. In seconds he is at the turn. Blinded by tears he clips through a fence and finally stops mired in the fresh dirt pile beside a grave in the cemetery. He collapses on the steering wheel banging his head over and over. "She's gone. Gone. My Angel is gone." Grief engulfs him and he sobs himself to sleep.

Next morning, a driver finds him and tries to help. But all Alex can do is cry, "I'm done. It's all done." The good Samaritan calls the police and Alex is taken to the hospital. He is examined but all he does is ramble and talk nonsense. A doctor diagnoses a psychotic break and they transfer him to the Selkirk Mental Hospital.

The week's startling Winnipeg Free Press headlines are all anyone can talk about:

Gimli House Explosion — Emergency Services Respond
Gimli House Explosion — Body Found in Debris

67

Rumble Riot Motorcycle Gang — Implicated in Gimli Gas Explosion

Gimli House Explosion — Linked to 30 year old Winnipeg Murder

Gimli Explosion, Johnson Murder, Rumble Riot — Bizarre Connections

Dr Heatherington signs the forms quickly, rattling off instructions to the nurse, "Patient is not responding to medication. We'll do the shock therapy in the morning. The usual prep please. Keep him quiet and comfortable tonight."

The nurse enters Alex's room, adjusts his blanket and checks his restraints. He is still but repeats over and over, "It's all gone. It's all gone. It's all gone." She lowers the lights and leaves.

Chapter Twelve — Alexander Comes Home

March 2007

One year later, Alex sits motionless on the couch looking around his house, the wreckage gone, the garbage gone. The only reminders are the two repaired holes in the wall. He looks at them trying to remember the anger and despair. Nothing. The gray hairs peppering his beard and hair make him appear older but the regular hospital meals have filled out some of the deep facial lines and his skin has a healthier tone.

Vivian, the home care worker sighs as she waits patiently for the toast to pop up. Alex can smell the coffee perking but the aroma doesn't elicit any response.

"Alex, breakfast is ready. Come to the table please."

Robot-like, Alex stands and obeys.

"Now let's get this toast down so you can take your pills."

Alex takes a bite of his toast then raises his coffee mug and takes a test sip.

"It's Meals on Wheels day so remember to let them in. It should be enough for the rest of the day. I've left sandwich meat and cheese in the fridge for you as well." She stands waiting for him to finish his toast so she can be on her way.

Finally the toast is eaten and she hands him his pills and water. He obediently swallows. "Okay, see you tomorrow." Alex responds by picking up his coffee mug and going back to the couch. He slowly sips his coffee, looks at the back door and says, "Bye." But the worker is long gone. His voice sounds loud in the void. *Silence is almost deafening if you think about it. Like a void. Odd word. What rhymes with void?*

Nothing. His mind moves like it's wallowing in molasses as he tries to form a line of poetry.

> Void of noise or ... sound ... no, no,
> My noise is all that fills my void ... mind ... no,
> no ...

Alex abandons the poem without regret…without feeling loss. The quiet fills him. *I guess this is better than the hospital. How long was I there? Too long. Months. So quiet. No crazies here. Just me I guess.* He looks out the window. *Snow. It's winter.* He opens the back door. Big flakes of snow drift softly down. The silence outside echoes the silence inside and he closes the door. *Mother. Nothing to say? So where are you when I need you? Need, maybe not need. Haven't needed you for a very long time. Guess it would be nice just to hear something, anything.* He sits back down on the couch and watches the snow fall.

The day passes. The meal is delivered. Alex opens doors and shuts them. He eats, visits the bathroom, sits and talks to his mother, eats, sits, goes to the bathroom and talks to his mother.

So Mother still not there? Where didja go? I know you're dead. The shrink told me you're dead. He couldn't hear you. He didn't hear the screaming and taunting. Only I heard that. Are you gone for good? Typical. Just when I need someone to talk you're gone. Pretty much the story of my life. He looks outside, sees nothing but darkness and goes to bed.

The month passes.

He opens the back door is surprised to see a robin. *Mother, it's spring.* The tiniest bit of something changes. He tries to

70

identify the feeling. But it moves off and he can't hold onto it. He turns around and sits back down again. *So Mother what should we talk about today?*

One April morning he opens the door and sees new green shoots of grass and a remembered feeling returns. This time it stays longer. He stands in the doorway wondering, feeling, breathing. *It's the air. Fresh. It feels fresh.* Not wanting to go back inside he steps out onto the grass and looks around. He sees his truck. *My truck. I wonder if it'll start? Mother let's go and see. Let's see if it starts. Keys, I need keys. Where are the keys Mother?*

The Meals on Wheels couple find him with his head under the hood of his truck talking to himself. They look quizzically at each other and the man says, "Alex we have your food. We'll just put it on the table, okay?" Alex looks up and nods. The man hurries inside and the kindhearted woman tries to engage Alex in conversation. Alex grunts and puts his head back under the hood. The man returns and they look at each other, "Okay Alex see you on Wednesday." No response. They head back to their car. "Well at least he's outside. First time in months. I'll take that as progress," the man says, "Wonder who he's talking to?"

By the middle of May, Alex has the truck running but is still hesitant to leave the yard. He sits in it every morning and explains how the engine works to his still silent Mother. His mind is foggy but he starts to walk around his yard and notice little projects that need attention. When it rains he is unhappy, there is nothing to do.

One morning Vivian brings in the Interlake Spectator and

leaves it on the table beside his toast and coffee. He picks it up and stares at the front page. A picture of a man and woman look back at him. Unsure he holds it closer and peers at the woman. "No. It can't be. She's dead." He puts the paper back on the table and tries to figure out what he saw. He picks it up again and touches the woman's face. "It's my Angel. It's Sigga. How can this be?" He looks at the face beside her. "Why is that bastard with her? What's going on?" He carefully reads each word out loud,

"LOCAL…MAN…SHORTLISTED…FOR… MAJOR…LITERARY...AWARD."

He slowly focuses on the writing underneath the picture and processes the words…'Steve Oddleifson and his wife recently returned from their Paris honeymoon and were overjoyed to hear of'…*Married! My Angel is married to that bastard. She's alive! Sigga's alive. She isn't dead. Mother look at this! Sigga's alive.* A smile forms and an unfamiliar feeling slowly fills his chest. He sits back and tries to recognize the feeling. The warmth grows stronger and he says to himself, *Joy? Joy. My Angel is alive. I have to think about this. Why can't I think? Everything is so hazy. Foggy. Think! My Angel's alive.*

Vivian stands over him with his pills and water. Alex looks at them, really seeing them for the first time. *The pills. The bloody pills. It's the pills.*

The worker says, "Alex, your pills. C'mon take your pills. I need to go. Got things to do. Take your pills." And she moves her hand closer.

Alex looks at the pills, *I can't take the pills. I won't take the pills.* He pushes her hand away and says, "No."

72

"Now Alex. You have to take your pills." Frustrated, she tries an empty threat. "You don't want to go back to the hospital now, do you?" And she pushes them closer.

He looks around trying to focus on a plan. *Can't take them. Can I pretend and hold them in my hand? Don't think that'll work.*

"Alex c'mon now. Take the pills. Hospital or pills, your choice."

He finally nods and takes the pills from her. He pops them in his mouth and takes the water. Satisfied, the worker prattles on as she leaves. The door closes and Alex spits the pills out into his hand. *Right, no more pills.* He looks lovingly at the picture of his Angel, gently touches her face. *My Angel is alive. Whatever the rest of this shit is, my Angel's alive.*

Two weeks later Alex refuses to let the Home Care Worker in. "Go to hell and take your hospital with you." When the Meals on Wheels is delivered he refuses to open the door and tells them where they can put their meals. Horrified, the couple flees.

Alex stands in front of his couch and looks around at his place. He says out loud, "So Mother, I got rid of all the do-gooders, it's just you and me now...and my Angel Sigga. Just a little problem, she married that asshole. That bloody Steve Oddleifson and his awards. Well I'm going to take that smile off his face."

Chapter Thirteen — Steve Oddleifson and Susie Campbell

Steve's toned muscles glisten in the morning sun as he shakes the water out of his sandy coloured hair. He scoops his towel from the beach and dries off as he walks up his side lawn. *It's so gorgeous...I think we'll have a fire after dinner.* He uprights the Adirondack chairs around the fire pit. *One missing...shoved in the caragana?...that's strange. I'm sure I put them all...* Steve pulls the chair out and turns it around, jumps...*Jesus!...*a raccoon grins up at him. *It isn't moving,* he moves closer, *it's dead! Geez, it's gutted, God, gutted!* The smiling, disemboweled raccoon sits propped up, staring.

Steve stands still. *This is deliberate...and sick...who'd do this? I'm calling Evan before I make up eight conspiracy theories. He'll help figure this out.* He turns towards the house. *Susie? She better not see this.* He drapes his towel over the chair and heads in.

The last few years have been kind to Susie. Her still youthful face glows with a golden tan and there are no traces of gray in the blonde. She restarts the laptop slide show and the album title displays: "Paris Honeymoon 2007". She smiles when a picture appears of her sitting in the Grand Gallerie at the Louvre, knitting. She laughs out loud when she remembers that day. *I'm no art lover but I have to say that those chubby, or rather Rubinesque ladies in the pictures were good company while Steve enjoyed the rest of the museum. Look at me Sigga, knitting! Can you imagine. Bless Jeannie for having the patience to teach me. I love it...stitch after stitch... creating something.* She leans back in her kitchen chair and thinks, *Dear Sigga, I miss you so much. I wish you could see*

74

how far I've come. Me, Susie Campbell, biker chick, Mrs Steve Oddleifson, recently returned from her Paris honeymoon. Paris for heaven's sake! Sigga, without you, I'd probably be dead. I owe you everything. Everything.

She looks at Steve coming through the deck door. *Wow! Look at him. We're in our fifties, he's still so fit, would he say that about me?* She adjusts the waist band on her shorts, *I better get more exercise.* "Morning Honey. You were up early. Have a good swim?"

Steve looks at her, his mind still filled by the raccoon. "Yeah...great...uh..."

"What's wrong...something's wrong." She jumps to her feet. "Are you hurt?"

"No, no, I'm fine. Just another sick joke." He walks to the coffee pot, pours a cup and picks up the phone. "Just a sec, Honey." He speed dials Evan.

Susie takes hold of his arm. "What's going on? Talk to me."

"Just a sec...Evan, are you busy?"

Susie listens to the one-sided conversation. "...got a little trouble here, could you come and look at it...Yes, now... That's okay?...Thanks." Steve hangs up, sips his hot coffee and says, "Okay Honey. Nothing to worry about. Evan's coming over. Some idiot killed a raccoon and put it on a lawn chair. Probably nothing, but it seems sinister. I want..."

"What? Why in the world..." She turns towards the deck door.

Steve catches her arm and steers her back to her coffee and laptop, tries to reassure her, "It's nothing. Evan's coming over and we'll handle it. I'm probably blowing it out of proportion."

Susie looks panicked.

He continues, "It's another sick joke, like the rat on the steps and the stinking fish on the deck."

Susie wrests her arm from Steve's hand, yells, "What the hell's going on!"

Steve tries to continue calmly, "Let's drink our coffee and wait for Evan. He'll know if it's time to get the police involved."

Susie exclaims, "Police! Could this be Rumble Riot? God, are they here?" She moves closer to Steve, looks outside.

Steve wraps her in his arms, holds her until she settles, whispers in her ear, "My love, the biker gang is in the past. We're safe. It's just a raccoon, a prank. Evan'll look at it and he'll know what, if anything we should do. Let's wait for him. Let's sit down and finish our coffee. Let's go over the plans for tonight."

Steve urges her to her seat and sits across from her. They pick up their cups and sip. Steve can see the worry on Susie's face. "We have great weather. Let's eat outside tonight, what do you think?"

Susie sucks in a slow breath and says, "Yeah, the dinner party." She thinks, *raccoon, dead, what the hell?* "We should cancel. Right?"

"No Honey. The raccoon is probably a lot of nothing. I'm looking forward to seeing everyone. So…the dinner party? What's next on your list?"

Susie stares at him. *Evan's coming, he's good, he'll help.* She reluctantly focuses on the plans. "The salad's ready, the rice casserole needs only an hour in the oven and the vegetables are all set up, ready to cook. That Chablis'll be excellent. " *What else, what else, damn raccoon, Evan'll help us.* She shakes her head. "Those gorgeous glasses from Jeannie and Ernie'll be perfect, love wedding presents. You're

76

in charge of the wine. Eating outside? We could dish up at the dining room table and take it out, simple, it'll work."

"We have great friends coming. Really looking forward to this."

Susie scans down the guest list. "It's too bad about Evan and his wife. Still can't believe they're separated."

"I know, surprised the heck out of me too."

"I really didn't know her that well. Has Evan said anything?"

Steve shakes his head. "Not a word."

Susie sighs and returns to her list, "You've known Ernie and Jeannie Baxter since high school, now I feel they're my friends too. Jeannie and I really hit it off through those years I claimed to be Sigga Johnson, and even after the truth came out she remained a good friend. Evan Boychuk, funny how things turn out, at one point I thought he was trying to put me in jail...Who are Jerry and Mavis Erikson? How do you know them?"

"I knew Jerry in school, but remember, I left Gimli in grade twelve. It's been decades. I remember him back then but really got to know him better at Rotary. I guess he wasn't at the Fireside you went to."

Susie's body tenses, *Oh my God, the night of the Fireside. Sigga's house exploding. Getting arrested.* She starts to shake.

"Honey don't go there. Sorry I mentioned the Rotary get-together. Nothing's going to touch you. Everything's good." He gently rubs her back.

Susie looks up at him and smiles weakly. "Okay sorry. What were you saying?"

"I was telling you about Jerry Erikson."

Susie tries to focus, "Right. What's he do?"

77

"He owns Erikson's Fish, just outside of town, good fish at a decent price…It's kind of exciting hosting our first party as mister and missus isn't it?"

"It isn't just our first party, it's a Way-to-Go party. It's not every day you're shortlisted for an Edgar Mystery Award. Very impressive. I'm so proud of you."

"Thanks Honey. We mustn't get ahead of ourselves, but you're right, being shortlisted is something to celebrate. And speaking of my books, last night I finally figured out what my next book is."

"Really? What?"

"Your story…it's a page turner…you, in the Rumble Riot biker gang, witnessing that murder and running to save your life, meeting Sigga…"

"Yeah, that's what saved me, meeting her."

She's about to launch into talking about Sigga but Steve smiles and steers the conversation back to his book, "Yes, Sigga was your guardian angel. You were sought by the FBI, you ended up impersonating Sigga Johnson back here in Gimli, you fell in love…"

"Okay, my life was an enthralling drama but writing about it…I don't know."

"…and then your amazing lawyer, Irving Spellman saving you. It's got romance, murder, police, gang violence, your house explodes! and the whole thing is one long chase. It's a hot story that'll sell millions — okay, thousands. It's a good story and I'd love to write it."

"But it's my story. It's my life and putting it in print is scary. I'm not sure…"

"And you get to approve everything. There won't be anything in this book that you don't want. And best of all, we'll be working together."

78

"My name won't be on the cover, will it? Not sure I want that."

"Don't worry, we can name you as a contributor in the front pages if you like."

Susie looks worried. "Not sure. Let me think about it, okay? I'll have final say on everything?"

Steve smiles and nods, "Absolutely, I won't do anything you don't want."

"I've got to think about this. There's too much going on right now." She stops and groans. "And I've got that interview for the volunteer job at the Women's Resource Center tomorrow. I should cancel that."

"No you should not. This is nothing but a bit of mischief. You need to get out and what better way than to volunteer for something as valuable as the Center. You have a lot of experience to share. What'd the ad say again?'

"Volunteer intake person needed at the Women's Resource Centre. They want help taking calls from clients and then passing them on to whoever can help. It's kinda like a hot line I guess."

"Okay. Agreed? You will go?"

Reluctantly, Susie takes a deep breath and nods.

"Good for you. You coming for a swim?"

"No. Go get wet." Still looking conflicted she puckers and blows him a kiss as he heads out.

Retired Winnipeg Police Captain Evan Boychuk strides into the backyard, still military trim but now shockingly gray. His still dark eyebrows slash across an unlined face. He looks purposely around and heads over to the fire pit, leans down and pulls the raccoon's stomach fur back with a stick. "Where was the chair when you found it?"

Evan follows Steve over to a caragana bush. "Not a lot of disturbance here. Looks like two sets of prints." He looks at

79

Steve's feet. "Your bare feet and a pair of shoes. Could be an older kid having fun. Seems a bit extreme but really nothing criminal. You've also found a rat on the front steps and dead fish on the deck? This is more than a coincidence...It's understandable you're disturbed." They go up on the deck and sit down.

"Evan, how worried should I be about this? Have you ever seen anything like this?"

Evan pauses, then says, "Steve, after thirty years with the police I've pretty much seen it all. This is worth being concerned about, but there's no clear threat to you or Susie. If I were you, I'd put in some of those cameras, front and back. As for police? Not a bad idea to alert them that this is happening and you're uneasy about it. But there's not much they can do. Let's take some pictures, and you have to keep a record from now on. Start a journal, the dates, a bit of detail. After the pics we can get rid of Mr Raccoon before the party."

Chapter Fourteen — The Writing on the Window

The evening is perfect. Two pelicans float near shore, slowly rising and falling on the gentle swell. A warm breeze drifts across the deck, just enough to keep the mosquitoes quiet. Dinner is finished and the friends sit, contented, looking out onto the lake.

Ernie Baxter absently rubs his paunch and then breaks the silence, "I have one question, why are Steve and Susie the only couple with lake front property?"

Evan Boychuk laughs and says, "Because we're all idiots."

Ernie's wife Jeannie's petite frame is swallowed in a deck chair. She looks past her husband at Steve. *We dated in high school, back then I thought he was special and look at him now…an author.* She raises her wine glass, "Here's to our famous author, Steve Oddleifson." The others raise their glasses, "To Steve…"

Steve holds up his hand. "Yes, thanks once again. I agree it's a coup, but let's not count our chickens just yet. The book's shortlisted, but still a long shot. I like that it's happened, but I still can't believe it."

Evan says, "Being shortlisted is an honour in itself. You've earned this Steve, enjoy it."

Jerry shakes his shaggy red head and says, "I didn't know you were a writer."

"Well, when I started writing I wanted to be anonymous so I used a pen name."

Jerry's wife Mavis stretches her long legs and comments, "Imagine you being Kathe Richard. I've read all your mysteries and would never have known you were a man."

81

Evan openly stares at Mavis, admiring her legs, then mentally quashes his reaction, *Not single yet.*

Steve looks over at Mavis and says, "Thanks Mavis, that's a compliment."

Mavis continues, "Is there any significance to that name?"

"As a matter of fact, Kathe's my mother's name and Richard's my father's."

Mavis smiles. "A nice tribute."

Ernie says, "And now you're living your own little mystery." He turns to Evan, "What do you make of it all Evan?"

Jerry sits forward and asks, "Mystery? What mystery?"

Steve shakes his head. "We've had a few dead animals around the place but the last one was obviously gutted and posed. Really creepy! Don't know what to make of it. Evan has suggested a security camera and I'm going to look into that on Monday."

Jerry says, "Good Lord! Have you gone to the cops?"

"Evan took some pics and I'll talk to the RCMP on Monday. Evan says there isn't much they can do except maybe patrol a little more. So we'll see."

Concerned, Jerry asks, "Have you noticed anybody out of the ordinary around here?"

"Well, there's you…"

Everyone laughs, then Steve continues, "No, not really. But since this morning I've been on the alert. Take for instance that boater out there. He's been there for hours. I'm becoming suspicious of everything."

Evan asks Steve, "Got binoculars?" Steve shakes his head and Evan jumps up. "I've got a pair in the car, just a sec."

Back quickly, he hands them to Jerry. "You're the fisherman around here, you look."

82

Jerry adjusts the focus. "Oh yeah, that's a guy that sells me fish, Alex Gislason. He's okay. An oddball, bit of a loner but harmless. Probably likes to fish that spot. He started working for us decades ago, when my dad ran Erikson's Fish."

Steve looks quizzically at Jerry, "I don't recognize that name. Would I know him?"

Jerry shakes his head slowly and says, "He was a few years ahead of us in school so it's not likely."

"Like I said, I'm becoming suspicious of everything."

Ernie says, "Probably some kids having fun. Kinda really bad taste but you don't know what the little buggers'll get up to these days."

"Probably, but for peace of mind I'm getting a security system installed as soon as possible."

Susie stands and glances around the group. *It's time for a change of topic.* "Anyone for more coffee? How about more cake?"

Jeanie stands and looks at Mavis. The two women go to help Susie in the kitchen.

Half a mile off shore the wind picks up and starts the skiff rolling and bucking. The grizzled man curses and mutters as he pulls in his net. *Bastard. Lording it over his friends in his fancy house. Should be my house, my friends, my woman, my life. Who does he think he is? Lord of the manor. Yeah right! God damn bastard. That's what he is. He has it all — money, woman, house, career, everything. I have nothing. Nothing! He'll get his. I'll make sure he gets his. Bastard! We'll see who's the bastard.*

Susie watches Steve sleep. *God I love this man.* She traces his

83

lower lip with her forefinger. Steve playfully nips at her.

"Oh, you brat, how long've you been lying there pretending to be asleep?"

Steve stretches. "Not long. Wonderful party last night. You did great."

"Thanks Honey. You too. We have great friends. The food seemed to be a hit. And the weather sure cooperated. I'm so glad you asked the Eriksons. I like Jerry and Mavis. I was quite startled to see Jerry. If he'd worn a helmet he'd look just like a marauding Viking."

"Funny you should say that because that's exactly what he is every year in the Icelandic Festival Parade."

Susie smiles. "And didn't you love Evan's new car? Wow, a Lexus! It's pretty nice isn't it?"

Steve laughs. "You angling for a new car?"

"No, I love my BMW. I was thinking you might like a change from your Corvette. It's getting on and keeps going into the garage for this or that."

"God no! My Vette's a classic, thank you very much."

"But it's a money pit! I guess it's something I just don't get. Tell me again, why do you have it?"

"The Vette only gets used in the summer and then only a bit around town and if I'm lucky, the odd parade. And yes, I know it costs, but I enjoy owning a classic. It's my baby."

Susie laughs and sits up. "What are your plans for the day?"

Steve stretches and says, "I'm going to do a little research on security cameras and then I thought we could take a drive in the Vette, maybe dinner at Hecla?"

"That sounds great, my interview shouldn't take too long, I'm thinking maybe noon, one at the latest. I'll go put the coffee on. Let's have it on the deck. It looks gorgeous out."

"Okay. Put on your suit and we can swim after. Your turn to make breakfast."

Steve ogles her as she slips into her bathing suit and heads for the kitchen. She calls back at him, "C'mon sleepyhead, out of bed."

Steve thinks, *I'm a lucky man.*

Susie fills the coffee maker and measures the coffee carefully into the paper filter. To keep herself focused, she counts out loud, "One, two, three…" Once the machine is on she picks up her phone, walks into the living room. "Steve, there's a message from Jeannie, they want us to…" Susie looks up and screams, "STEVE!"

Steve rushes into the living room and stops, stunned, reads the backward image of scrawled black letters on a window.

U R
THE
BASTARD

He turns to a shaken Susie. "We have to call the RCMP. Now."

Steve and Evan stand beside each other in the living room watching Constable Hendricks take a picture of the window and then walk down onto the beach to inspect the area. Susie, wrapped in a blanket on the sofa, is wide-eyed and quiet.

Steve says, "Thanks for coming, Evan."

Evan nods. "Not much I can do but stand beside you and watch."

"What do you think's going on here? Who could be doing this?"

"Well you've obviously pissed someone off."

"Yeah, but you'd think I'd remember doing that. Here he comes."

Hendricks walks in. He takes a second look at Evan. *Hey, that's Inspector Boychuk. What's a retired bigwig doing here?* He nods at Evan, turns to Steve and says, "Nothing much out there. Looks like whoever did this covered his tracks pretty good. We'll put this in the file with the raccoon incident. We'll step up patrols in the area but other than that there's not much we can do. If you think of anyone who could be responsible for something like this, call us right away. Sorry Mr Oddleifson, but there's not a lot we can do. I'm off now." Hendricks nods towards Evan then refocuses on Steve, "Call if there are any more incidents."

Steve says, "I'll show you out."

The two men leave the room.

"Evan."

"Yes, Susie?"

"Do you think this could have anything to do with my past?"

Evan sits down beside her. "No I don't. If this was aimed at you I think they'd've written 'bitch', don't you?"

"I guess. This all makes no sense. We just got home. We haven't been anywhere or done anything to upset anyone. Makes no sense."

"You let me and Steve and the RCMP deal with this. Try not to worry. We'll catch these weirdos."

Steve comes back and sits across from Evan and Susie. "Well, I can see they can't do much but I feel better for involving them. Looks like vandalism…maybe a bit more nasty but what can we do?"

Evan says, "We can get right on that security system. I'll help keep an eye out for the next few days until we can get those cameras in. Okay?"

86

"Thanks Evan. You're a good friend. Susie and I really appreciate it. Don't we Honey?"

Susie looks back at him, haunted.

Steve's heart aches as she nods. "Everything is going to be fine. Stop worrying. It's just some kids having a laugh at our expense."

Evan stands. "I guess I'll be going. I'll come over later this evening and we can work out a surveillance plan."

"Thank you so much Evan, we'll talk later on." Steve walks him to the door and returns to find Susie pacing the living room.

"We can't just sit here and do nothing Steve. I don't like any of this. It's scary. Who can have it in for us? What have we done? We have…"

Steve stops her and urges her back on the couch. Susie looks up at him, still agitated. "I'm canceling my appointment. I can't deal with one more thing today."

Steve sits down beside her. "We can't blow this out of proportion. It's probably nothing. Are we going to let a bunch of punks interfere with our lives? No. You'll feel better after a swim and breakfast. I think you have to go to your appointment. We're going to find this is just kids thinking they're funny. It has nothing to do with your past. Right?"

Susie appears to waver. She finally says, "You're probably right but it's unnerving. I don't like it."

"And I don't either. But let's continue with our plans and have a nice day. Okay?"

"Okay, let's swim first and then I'll make us a good breakfast and then I'm going to knock their socks off in my interview."

Relieved, Steve laughs, "You bet you are."

87

Chapter Fifteen — The Interview

"Please call me Joan." Joan Pullman sits down behind her desk. "So, you've been in Gimli since 2004 and you're recently married, two months ago. Let's talk a little about your history and what experience you can bring to the Centre."

"Okay. The quick version, I was born in LA. I was abused by my family and ran away at age fifteen. I worked lots of low end jobs and finally hooked up with a guy in the Rumble Riot, the biker gang, the one that's in the news all the time. I saw, took part in and had done to me everything you can imagine. I was caught planning to leave the gang, so they made me witness a brutal murder and created evidence that I did it. I ran anyways. The Riot was after me and so were the FBI, who wanted me as a witness, but I thought they wanted me for the murder.

"In Chicago I met a woman, Sigga Johnson. We ran from both the Rumble Riot and the FBI down into Texas. Just before Sigga died of cancer she insisted I assume her identity and take over her house here in Gimli. Finally the FBI and the Rumble Riot caught up with me. The Riot blew up my house and the FBI had me arrested by the RCMP. A wonderful lawyer, Irving Spellman, sorted it out and all the charges were dropped. I met Steve. We married and now I'm sitting here."

Mrs Pullman, a little stunned, looks down at the papers on her desk and gathers her thoughts for a moment. She finally says, "That's quite a story. I have to commend you for surviving. Do you think your history'll help you understand the problems the women who come to the centre have?"

"Without Sigga Johnson's help I would not be sitting here. I owe her my life. I want to pay that back in whatever small way I can. There isn't much I haven't experienced or seen. I'm sure that I can use that to help someone."

"Tell me about the abuse you suffered as a child."

Susie sits up straight, sucks in a breath and starts, "It was an uncle. He had a withered arm and was on 'disability'. He couldn't work because of the pain and lived in the back room."

"What would happen?"

"Mom and Dad'd get drunk or go to a movie or the bar. They were often out..." Susie's mouth opens and she stares off. "He'd catch me by the wrist and twist my arm behind my back. I'd end up on the floor held by his legs. He'd rip off my blouse and panties...he'd...then..." Susie's face freezes in terror, her breath comes in shallow pants.

"Thank you Susie. I've heard different variations of that same story over and over. You're not alone. Tell me about your husband, Steve."

Susie smiles and starts to breathe normally. "He believed in me right through it all. I've been so lucky."

"Susie, have you had any counselling to help you with all this baggage?"

"No. I've always just looked after myself."

"Here at the Centre we have many resources. You might be able to use one of our psychologists to help you with issues about your past. Would you like me to set up an appointment?"

"Do you really think I need that? I was thinking I'd be a help for others."

"Helping yourself first would be another asset for your work here. I think you would be a valuable addition to our

89

Centre but we all have things worth talking about and some of them are things that rear their heads when you least expect."

Susie's face contorts, her tears well up, she drops her head into her arms and weeps. Joan stands up and sits beside her, hugs her shoulder. She pulls several tissues from the ever present box and slips them into Susie's hand. The sobbing gentles into sniffles. The interviewer returns to her chair.

Susie sits up, wiping her face. After a few calming breaths she says, "Yes. I think perhaps an appointment or two might help."

Joan smiles reassuringly, looks at her computer screen and writes two dates on an appointment card. "Will these dates work for you?"

"Yes, thank you, these dates'll be fine. I understand I might not be ready to help others yet. Maybe some day."

"That's the spirit. When you're ready I'm sure you'll be one of the best."

"Thank you. You'll be seeing me again."

Susie pulls her BMW into the drive and stops. *What do I say to Steve? How about the truth, yeah, that's the best, the truth.*

Inside, Steve lays down his book and turns to Susie as she enters. "So how'd it go? Get the job?"

"Not exactly."

Steve looks puzzled, "Huh?"

"I met the nicest woman, Joan Pullman. She was great. She convinced me that I need some counselling before I can help other women. And she's right. She set up a few counselling appointments to help me work through all my stuff. Seems I'm not ready to help others yet, and I agree. But I'll work on this and keep in touch with them and in the end, I think that's the place where I should be helping others."

Steve takes a second to absorb it all, then says, "I'm so proud of you. Anything I can do to help, just ask. Come here." He pulls her into a hug.

Chapter Sixteen — Alexander Overhears

Alexander brakes hard and the toolbox slides forward on the seat. "Damn!" He grabs the edge just in time. He looks up, sees Mavis entering the Erikson's Fish filleting shed. "Shit!" *Guess I'll sit a while. Damn woman always wants to know something. Can't just say nothin'. Gotta go on about 'How are you doing? How's fishing? Isn't the weather wonderful?' Drives me nuts.* He drums his fingers on the steering wheel, looks at his watch and mumbles, "This is getting me nowhere. C'mon old lady. Get a move on." He snorts. *Can't sit all day. Maybe she won't remember me, it's been a while — fat chance.* He gets out and hefts the fish box from the cargo deck. As he nears the shed door he hears Mavis, "...Steve and Susie. I think they..." He stops, steps back and leans against the wall to listen.

"Jerry, are you listening to me?"

"Sorry Dear, what did you say again?"

"I ordered flowers to thank Steve and Susie for the lovely dinner and of course to congratulate Steve on being shortlisted. What's that mystery prize called again?"

"The Edgar."

"Right. What an odd name."

"I think it has to do with Edgar Allan Poe."

"Oh my God, that weird guy. Those horror movies?"

"Mavis, those were movies based on his books, mystery books."

"Well, whatever. They were scary as hell."

"You were saying you ordered flowers?"

"Yes I did. Okay with you?"

"Sure. Anything else? I'm kinda busy here."

"Yes, there is. I was thinking about those security cameras Steve's getting. I think we could use some here. One around your shed and one at the house. It would help me monitor who's driving up in the yard. You can't be too careful these days. Look at Steve and Susie."

"Yeah, I was thinking the same thing. I could pop down to Wave Electronics this afternoon if I can ever finish work here."

Mavis laughs. "Okay okay, I can take a hint."

Alexander jumps. *She'll catch me listening!* He moves towards the door and almost collides with Mavis on the way out.

"Alex, good to see you. You've been gone a long time...Hope things are going well for you. How are you?"

Alexander pushes past her.

Mavis shakes her head. *A year in Selkirk and he's just as weird as ever.*

Alexander shoves the money he got for the fish into his shirt pocket and throws the empty fish box into the back of his truck. In the truck he sits motionless for a few seconds. Through clenched teeth he curses, "God damn, God damn. God damn. Cameras. Shit!"

He speeds out onto the highway, yelling, "Damn it! Cameras! There goes my little game. No more dead fish for Steve. Shit! And the Edgar, yeah...a Bastard award. He's got it all and I got nothing. I'll get him."

He checks the speedometer and slows down. Muttering, he continues on to South Beach, pulls into his driveway. "Damn! That Bastard!" He steps inside, looks around. With one sweep he clears off the kitchen table, sending the dishes and the remains of breakfast flying around the room. He grabs

93

a can of beer out of the fridge, flops on his couch and snaps open the tab.

He mutters, "Jesus Christ. That bastard has everything. What more can he get? He has my life. He has my woman. He has success. Jesus. He has my success." Anger builds, fills his whole body. He downs his beer, crushes the can in his hand, *I have to do something...He can't have it all...I've waited and waited...He just keeps getting more and more...When's it my turn? For God's sake, when's it my turn?* He grabs another beer from the fridge and flops back on the sofa. He takes a slug, rummages for the TV remote and settles back to watch.

The figures on the screen aren't registering. In his mind are visions of Steve accepting his award, smiling and waving. *Damn it. I've gotta wipe that smile off his ugly face.* Between slugs of beer, he mouths over and over, *smother him, choke his ugly face, smother him, make him pay, it's my house, my money, Sigga's mine...*

Ruby screams in his head. ***You do something? Don't make me laugh. You're useless! Useless. Do you hear me you lazy lump of nothing. Do something? Right!***

Alexander grabs his ears trying to shut her out. "Now you come back? Shut up Mother!"

Useless, useless, useless.

Slowly shaking his head he mumbles, "For months I begged you to talk to me and you wouldn't. Now, leave me alone you old bitch!" He jumps up, plugging his ears. "La la la la la la," he chants.

You'll never be half the man Steven is. Not half. You're no good, no good. It's all your fault. Do you hear me? It's all your fault!

Alexander screams, "Leave me alone, leave me alone." He runs over to the wall and bangs his head.

Her voice gets louder. *Idiot, idiot, good for nothing. Why don't you do something?*

He slams his fist through the wallboard then looks at his bleeding hand in wonder. Driving pain assaults him. Waves of fire replace Ruby's voice and he starts laughing, holding his bleeding hand in the air, dancing around on his broken dishes. To the ghost of his mother he yells, "Bitch! I'll make him pay. You'll see!"

Chapter Seventeen — Poor Little Larry

Larry Musgrove walks out of his yard onto Fifth Avenue. His mother calls to him, "Watch for cars Larry, you're my little Larry, I only have one little Larry."

"I will Mommy." His pudgy hand straightens his hat as he walks onto the road. A butterfly catches his eye. "Pretty." He starts to follow, but hears voices behind him. "Hi Mrs Carson. Are you watching for cars? Mommy says to watch for cars."

"Hi Larry. Yes, I'm watching for cars."

"I got a new hat." He pulls off his sky blue camp hat with big black letters and says, "Look it says 'Larry', right?"

Mrs Carson smiles. "That's a great hat. You won't lose that with your name on it. Are you going to the playground?"

"Yes. Mommy says watch for cars and go straight to the playground. Wanna watch me go to the playground?"

Mrs Carson's companion looks at her. "Is there something…"

Shaking her head, Mrs Carson whispers, "Later."

"We're walking right past the playground, we'll watch you go in." The three walk a bit down the road. "Here we are. You go in now."

Larry smiles and waves. "Bye, Mrs Carson. It was nice walking together."

She waves and says quietly to her friend, "Poor little Larry. He was very ill, had an extremely high fever when he was about four. The doctors think his brain stopped developing at that point."

"What a shame. He has such a sweet face. Someone must love him very much, look how nicely he's dressed. How old is he?"

"He's eight now. He's an only child and his mother dotes on him. Lovely child, wouldn't hurt a fly."

They watch Larry go over to three boys playing in the sand box and then they move on down the street.

One boy is building roads with a scratched up dump truck. A skinny kid has built up a mound and yells, "Toboggan slide!" The third boy, much shorter than the other two, says, "Hey, that's where my gravel pit's going." The road builder grabs his truck and stands up, catches sight of Larry. "Retard, whatcha looking at?"

The other boys stand. "Yeah, Retard, whatcha looking at? Get lost. Scram!"

Larry hesitates and a handful of sand hits his face. Scared, he tries to move but can't. He looks down at his feet. The boys move towards him. Frantically Larry urges his feet to move. They get close and his feet come alive, his chubby legs churn. He reaches the gate, struggles with the latch until it springs open. Panicking he runs through and dives behind a bush. He looks back and is relieved to see the boys have returned to the sand box.

His angelic face screws up. "All I want is…" A flash of orange distracts him. "Kitty. Here kitty, kitty." He follows the feline through a yard and out onto Fourth Avenue. The cat heads south, just out of reach.

Alexander swills the last of his beer, clunks the empty on the bar and leaves. Stepping out of the Oldie he cringes in the blinding sun. "Christ!" He shades his eyes, heads to his truck, opens the glove compartment and feels around for his sun glasses. *Son of a bitch.* Finally finds them.

A vintage red Corvette slips slowly past. He whistles. Now that's a car! It slides like a sleek panther onto the lot of M & J Auto. He's about to drive off when Steve Oddleifson gets out of the Corvette and saunters into the office.

97

"Jesus H Christ! Really! A Corvette! There's nothing that fucker doesn't have!"

Alexander slams into first and roars down Centre Street. "Damn! Damn! DAMN!" I'll get that bastard.

He turns left onto Third Avenue and Ruby starts screaming, *I told you you're worthless. You have nothing and never will.*

"For Christ sake, Mother, butt out."

Ruby laughs. *Worthless, worthless, that's what you are! You're an idiot. You do nothing right. You're worthless.*

Alexander drives through the stop sign at the laundromat, screaming, "Leave me the fuck alone. I watched you die. Now go away! Did you see that smug asshole with his bloody Corvette? That should be my car. My car. This is all your fault."

What an idiot. You don't deserve a car like that. Look at you. Loser. You're a Loser!

Alexander's truck leans through the turn at the end of Third Avenue. "Get outta my head, damn it!"

The cat stops and looks back at Larry. Larry is encouraged. "Nice kitty. Here kitty kitty. Wanna hug kitty? C'mere kitty." The cat sniffs the air and picks up speed.

Larry hears a car and looks back. "Uh-oh, a car. Watch for cars. Mommy says watch for cars. Kitty watch for cars." Larry hurries to the ditch all the while calling, "Kitty, car! Watch for cars!" The cat looks straight ahead and runs along the government ditch. The car passes. Larry leaves the ditch and follows the cat as it turns down South Colonization Road.

Barely in control, Alexander's truck turns onto Colonization. Horrified, he screeches to a stop. Little Larry stands motionless in front of the truck and bursts into tears.

Alexander freezes. *My God, I could have killed him.* He rolls down his window and yells, "For Christ's sake kid, stop crying!" Larry cries louder. He gets out, grabs Larry by the shoulders and gives him a shake. Wide-eyed, Larry gulps and stops crying. "Now listen kid, you shouldn't be on the road…" Larry starts to wail.

Alex thinks, *I gotta shut him up.* "Hey kid, you wanna ride in my truck?"

Larry stops crying and looks at the truck, nods.

"Okay then, c'mon. Let's go for a ride."

He helps Larry into the cab and jumps in. "Hold on kid." He laughs. "You like trucks, kid?"

Larry nods and leans forward to see out the windshield.

"Me too. Always wanted one when I was a kid. Pretty cool truck eh?"

Larry smiles. "Cool truck. You see my kitty?"

"Nope. You gotta cat?"

Larry shakes his head. "No. Wanna kitty."

"Kid you don't want no stinking cat. You wanna dog. Now that's a pet. Not some stinking cat."

Larry looks at Alexander and screws up his face. "I wanna kitty."

Alexander sees he's about to cry and says, "It's okay kid. You wanna cat, you can have a cat."

Larry smiles and looks happily out the windshield.

Relieved, Alexander settles back and changes gear. "Let's have some fun." He floors it. Larry falls back in the seat and bursts out crying.

"Oh for Christ's sake kid, don't start crying again."

Larry looks at him, mouth wide. "Maaaaa…aaaaaa…"

"Shut the fuck up!"

Louder, "Bahhaaaaa…"

99

"God...shut up, shut up, shut up!"

Out on Highway 9 now, Larry wails.

"For fuck's sake, stop your screaming."

Ruby starts in again, *Look at you, you useless piece of shit. Scaring a kid. What a loser.*

"Shut up...both of you!"

Alexander makes a right turn onto the first gravel road he comes to. He slams on the brakes. He grabs his head and squeezes. *God, my head. I'm gonna explode!* He grabs Larry. "Stop this crying kid or I'll give you something to cry about." He shakes him harder and Larry screams louder.

His mother screams, *You idiot! What a loser.*

Larry's eyes bug out in terror, he arches his back, howls.

Alexander puts his hand over Larry's mouth but the screams keep coming. "Shut the fuck up! Stop it!" He wraps his hands around Larry's throat and squeezes. The noise weakens, then grows thinner.

Mother yells, *You loser. You're a loser.*

He squeezes harder, harder, harder...finally nothing. Larry's plump body slumps and Ruby is silent. Alexander releases his hands. Silence. He collapses back in the seat. Relief.

He looks at Larry's body. "What've I done? Shit, shit shit." Terrified, he looks around to see if anyone saw. *Alone, good.* He leans back and closes his eyes. *Shit, I've killed animals, but never a kid.* Eyes closed, he sits quietly for a while. *What am I gonna do? A body.* An idea forms and he smirks. "I know just where I'm putting you."

He spreads a tarp in the cargo bed, then gets Larry's body. He looks around, pulls him out of the cab and dumps him on the tarp. He picks up the hat off the cab floor, wraps it with

100

the limp body and looks around again...*so far so good. I'll have to wait until dark. Now home...then beer.*

He turns the truck and heads to South Beach. He backs up close to his door, gets out and walks out to the road, checks his neighbours on both sides, *all clear.* He pulls tarp-wrapped Larry out of the truck, hurries inside and throws the bundled body on his bed. He gets a beer.

Plan, gotta have a plan...Okay, as soon as it's dark I'll take my bundle and put it where it'll cause the most trouble. He laughs, downs the rest of the can then snaps the tab off another.

As evening creeps in, Alexander gets drunker and more excited. *I'm going to wipe the smile off that bastard Steve's face once and for all. Who does he think he is? I'm older, I'm smarter. Everything he has should be mine. Sigga's mine. I saw her first. She's my Angel, my beautiful Angel Sigga. He doesn't des*erve her.

Ruby starts taunting, ***You're an idiot. Look at you. You're nothing.***

"God, Mother, Back again? Bitch, get outta my head. This is all your fault."

Loser, loser, loser. You can't do anything right. Who do you think you are?

Alexander presses his hands against his ears, "Shut up, Bitch."

You, make a plan? Forget it. You can't do anything right. You're a loser.

Alexander paces back and forth, moaning. "Get outta my head. Piss off Mother." Ruby screams, Alexander squeezes his head, screams, "God, the pain! The pain!" *I can't stand it anymore. Gotta get rid of you Mother. I know how to get rid of you.* He lifts Larry's body and carries it out to the shed, throws it on the filleting table. He pulls the tarp open and looks down at the still body.

101

Ruby starts again. *You idiot. What're you gonna do? You can't get rid of me. You're a loser. You're an idiot.*

Reeling, he looks at Larry. *I'll rip your heart out Steve...*

Ruby screams, *Idiot!*

Alexander laughs and rips Larry's shirt open. *I'll make you just like the raccoon.* He plunges the filleting knife into his gut. He sucks in a breath then looks at Larry's face, still, clean, oddly peaceful. His hand stops, still holding the knife... *I can't...I can't do this...*

Ruby falls silent. *Thank God, she's gone.*

He looks at the knife, then at Larry. *Yeah, just like the raccoon...but you aren't a raccoon are you?*

He returns to the house and gets another can of beer...*Get rid of the body and frame Steve at the same time...Yes, that bloody car of his. Yes, in the trunk, yeah, good, it'll work. Now, wait till everyone has gone to bed.* Smiling, he sits back and takes a long pull on his beer.

As the pile of empty cans beside the fridge grows, the clock hands slip past 3 AM. *Now's the time.* He goes out, wraps Larry carefully in the tarp and gently places the bundle back on the cargo deck of his truck. *What else, what else?* He checks around his scattered tools and picks up his slim jim. *Might need this.*

Minutes later Alexander pulls in beside Steve's Corvette at the M & J Auto lot. *Be quick, look natural, be smooth.* He slides in the slim jim, hooks the lever and pops the door lock. He pulls the trunk release and retrieves Larry's corpse. He hooks Larry's wrists into the trunk lid frame with zip ties. *Good, open the trunk, Larry opens his arms.* He closes the trunk quietly and is off.

102

Now for the final touch. Alexander drives past Steve's place and pulls in at the beach access. He takes the tarp and Larry's hat and walks back along the beach. At Steve's place he stands on the beach for several minutes and watches, looks closely. *No cameras on the house, the trees, the deck railings, none anywhere. Good, not installed yet.* He slips through the dark to the back deck and stuffs the tarp and Larry's hat under the steps. *Done. Good work Alex. Let's see you get out of this, you bastard.*

Chapter Eighteen — The Search for Larry

Riiing! Riiing!

Steve rolls over, looks at the clock and groans. *6:30! Who the hell?*

Susie half sits up and blinks. "God, what time is it?"

Steve fumbles with the phone, checks who's calling and says, "Jeannie this better be good."

"Sorry to call so early, but I thought you'd want to know. Little Larry Musgrove has been missing since yesterday afternoon. His mother and neighbours've been searching most of the night. The coast guard zodiac's searching the shoreline and there's a meeting this morning at the town hall, 7:30, to plan an organized search. I'll be there but Ernie's working. Evan already knows."

"Okay, thanks, see you there." He presses 'end call' and turns to Susie. "Who's Larry Musgrove? Jeannie thinks I know who he is. He's gone missing and everyone's meeting to organize a search."

"Oh no, not poor little Larry. He's the sweetest boy. Challenged. His mother's a single mom. She must be frantic. We're going, right?"

Steve scratches his head and nods. "I have to pick up the Corvette this morning but there's time. So let's shake a leg. You want to shower first?"

"No, you go first. I'll put the coffee on."

Steve and Susie pull up in front of the Town Hall. The area is already packed.

Sargent Phillips stands on the bottom step of the hall, addressing the crowd, "Larry Musgrove is a short, husky eight

104

year old who is mentally challenged. He's wearing blue pants, a light green t-shirt and a sky blue camp hat that says 'Larry'. Look where you'd expect to find a child, anywhere a child could fit. Be thorough. Report anything that seems significant to your team leader. And team leaders, report to the detachment at the end of your group's search. The constables are sorting people into search teams and assigning zones."

Jeannie motions Steve and Susie over. "I've already volunteered you. We've got the Loni Beach area." She nods towards Evan. "Evan's our captain."

He greets Steve and Susie with, "Now we're all here. We have the Loni Beach area to search. Let's meet at Steve's place. We can make our plan there. Let's say, fifteen minutes. That okay with you all?"

Steve says, "I have to pick up my car. I'll meet you at our house. If you've started out when I get there, I'll find you."

Steve pulls his classic car into his garage as Evan starts off with his section of the group. Jeannie says to the remaining people, "We'll start at the government ditch and work our way north. Evan's group's doing the beach area so it's just the street, yards and outbuildings. Evan says he'll meet us back here. I guess it makes the most sense if we split and half of us do one side of the street and the other half the opposite side. Hope no one minds my dog. Who knows, she may help." Jeannie's Akita, Chika, prances proudly ahead.

Three hours later, tired and disappointed, the searchers disband at Steve's driveway. Evan is heading for his car when Steve stops him. "Let's pick up a pizza and talk."

"Sounds great, but I have to report to the RCMP. I'll be right back, count me in."

105

Jeannie turns towards Steve. "I'm in too, but I'll take Chika home."

Susie says, "Jeannie, I love that dog. She can stay. It'll be okay. You can help me get things started."

"Okay, but she can be a handful."

Susie smiles. "Not a problem. It's nice having animals around. And we'll be outside. She can run around and be happy. I'll get her some water."

The pizza boxes are almost empty, the friends lean back in chairs on the deck, chatting quietly. Chika chases a seagull off the beach, then disappears around the side of the house. Jeannie calls her. The dog reappears and looks at her mistress. "Chika come here." She obediently runs onto the deck, but circles back into the yard. Jeanie shakes her head and ignores her.

Steve asks, "What happens now Evan? Did the cops say anything?"

"Almost all the groups had reported by the time I got there, and so far, everyone came up empty-handed. The coast guard found nothing along the shoreline. They'll set up another search, but they need all the reports to come in. They'll notify the group leaders."

Jeannie says, "I guess they'll have to start looking farther out of town. I hate to think something awful's happened to Larry."

"Do you know Larry's mother well, Jeannie?" Susie asks.

"Not really. Well enough to talk to her, but I really don't know her." Chika barks and Jeannie laughs. "Quiet girl." Chika looks up at her and barks again, plunges her head back down, pulls and growls. Jeannie can only see her rump and wagging tail. "Good grief what are you doing?" She goes down the stairs. "Chika stop it." But Chika continues to growl and pull. Jeanie grabs her collar and shaking it, yells, "Chika, bad." Chika lets go but twists from Jeanie's hold and pushes her head back under the step.

Evan walks over and says, "Let me look. She's got something cornered there."

Evan bends down and peers under the step, reaches in and pulls out the tarp and then the hat. He turns the hat over and reads, "Larry". Jeannie gasps and looks at Evan. He pulls out his cell phone and speed dials the RCMP.

"Oh my God," Susie says, "What's going on, Evan?"

Jeannie holds up her hand and they wait for Evan to finish talking to the RCMP. "Okay they're on their way. Take the dog inside 'til we find out what's what."

Barely five minutes pass and a cruiser pulls into the drive.

Evan describes finding Larry's hat and the tarp. The Constable questions Steve who answers, "Never saw that tarp before." The constable seals both in separate evidence bags. Crime scene tape is secured to the steps and deck. Another RCMP cruiser arrives and Sergeant Phillips gets out. He talks with Evan, then joins the two constables searching the yard.

Finally, one officer comes over and says to Evan and Steve, "These items have to be taken into Winnipeg for analysis. We don't want any speculation so let's hold back on telling the world about this"

Steve and Evan nod and walk the officers to their cruiser.

Back inside, Evan holds his hand up. "Ladies, they aren't sure what's what and they're taking it all into the city for analysis."

Jeannie paces and asks, "I saw what you found, Larry's hat and a tarp. Is the tarp yours?"

Steve shakes his head, looks at Evan. "What do you think's happening?"

107

The group swings their attention to Evan. He realizes he's got to be frank. "That hat fits the description of Larry's perfectly. The tarp is not Steve's and how it got there is a mystery. Because of the hat, the tarp's likely connected to Larry somehow. Every time you're somewhere or handle something, you usually leave traces behind. That's why they put tape around the space where the tarp was. They'll come back and look for traces of how it got there. In Winnipeg they'll go over that tarp to see where it came from, what it's been used for. They've got a lot of work to do. We have to wait and stay out of the back yard."

Steve turns away from Evan. Jeanie sits down beside Susie. A confused Steve finally says, "None of this looks good for me. I don't know what's going on but we have to keep this very quiet until the police confirm things." The friends look at each other, unsure of what to say.

Chapter Nineteen — The Finding of Little Larry

"Maybe they'll call today." Susie paces back and forth between the sink and table.

"Honey, sit down. Thanks for the eggs, good breakfast. Nothing will be back from forensics yet. It all takes time and we can't sit here stewing about something we know is not connected to us. We're going to go ahead with life as if nothing's happened...Let the RCMP do their job. This isn't our problem...I'm taking your car in for an oil change. What're your plans for the day? I have to be back for 1:30. The guys are coming to install the cameras."

"I need my car. I was going for groceries this morning."

"Take my Vette. You love to drive it."

Susie's eyes light up. "We need softener salt. Is the trunk big enough?"

"Yes, but get carryout. It's too heavy for you."

Susie raises the garage door and wrinkles her nose. *This place stinks, needs a good cleaning. Hope it's not more dead animals.* She slips into the leather seat of the Vette. *Surprised he let me take it alone, this's a first.* She turns the key and the 360 horses spring to life with a satisfying roar. Susie smiles, appreciating the power. *That's an ugly smell. I'll tell Steve. I'll leave the door open to air it out, yeah, maybe it'll blow away.* She lowers the ragtop, shifts into reverse and eases off on the clutch. The Corvette majestically moves onto North Lake. With the breeze blowing through her hair and the sun warming her face, she smiles. *I feel like a Queen.* She drives carefully. *God, if I scratch it, he'll kill me.* Susie parks on the Sobey's lot and sighs with relief. She gets out and walks

109

inside.

Finished shopping, she picks the shortest line and is surprised when Evan pushes his cart in behind her. "I think this is the shortest line. Hate waiting." He laughs, "I know. I'm retired and supposedly have all the time in the world. Still hate wasting time."

"Yes, there's something about wasted time — it's so wasted." They both laugh, Susie continues, "Steve's having the cameras installed today. Surprised how long it's taken."

"I thought it was unnecessarily long too. We were just talking about the delay the other day. The store said they had trouble ordering them in."

Susie pays for her order and asks for carryout. The boy arrives as Evan's order is being bagged. The carryout boy pushes the trolley with the two bags of softener salt and Susie leads the way pushing her lightly laden cart. She goes to the driver side and pops the trunk release.

The boy pulls the trunk handle.

Two small arms swing up with the lid, a small head sits stiffly on slight shoulders, putrid air wafts. The carryout boy gawks, mouth agape, Larry's sightless eyes are sunken, staring. The carryout boy turns and throws up on the bags of salt. He steadies himself on the trolley, points, his eyes riveted on the car trunk. Susie steps towards the back of the car, looks into the trunk and passes out beside the dripping trolley.

A woman starts screaming as Evan steps out of the store. Her screams instantly attract a crowd that gathers around the rear of the Corvette. Evan steps to the front and looks into the trunk. He blanches. "Jesus." He grimaces at the eye-watering stench and closes the trunk lid. Grabbing his cell, he speed dials Sergeant Phillips' direct line. Decades of experience engage as he turns to the crowd and mechanically says,

110

"Please move back. I'm calling the RCMP. Now move back." He motions with his free hand for the crowd to back up.

Horrified, the crowd is silent. A woman, overcome, starts to moan. Another woman beside her starts crying. One man runs from the group and braces himself against the store wall, retches and then sinks to the sidewalk, breathing heavily.

"Sergeant Phillips...Yes, but this is official business. Major murder scene, Sobey's lot. Get here now."

He bends down and checks on Susie who is still unconscious on the asphalt. She comes to and he helps her to a sitting position. She tries to focus, then starts to cry. "That poor little boy, that poor little boy. Evan, he's in Steve's car. What's going on? Oh my God. What's going on?"

Evan motions a man over to help the carryout boy who is moaning and swinging his arms back and forth, trying to speak. "He's in shock, take him into the Sobey's office and keep him there until the RCMP arrive. Don't leave him alone."

Two RCMP cars pull up. Evan steps over and details everything that's happened. He asks if he can put Susie in the back of one of the squad cars and the constable nods.

The constables call for assistance and tape off a wide area around the Corvette. By the time they have cleared the onlookers an ambulance arrives. The detachment sergeant drives up with two more squad cars. He talks to the constables and Evan, then he sits in the squad car beside Susie and talks quietly. Evan squats at the open car door, holding her hand, trying to comfort her.

"Ma'am, are you alright? I'm Sergeant Phillips from the Gimli detachment. Can you answer a few questions?"

Susie nods, but continues to cry. "I'm sorry. I can't stop crying."

111

"That's okay...Now, did you drive the car from home?"

"Yes."

"And that would be where?"

"Forty-six North Lake Street."

"Where was the car kept at your home?

"In the garage."

"When was the last time anyone drove the vehicle?"

"My husband picked it up yesterday morning from M & J's. They were fixing the lights. What's going on? I just don't understand. Why is that poor little boy in our car? Who would do such a thing?" Susie starts to sob louder.

The Sergeant looks past Susie at Evan and arches his brow.

Evan nods. "I can confirm that. Our group was heading to Steve's place to start a search of the Loni area. He left us to pick up his car, drove it home and joined us for the search."

"Okay. This lady needs medical attention. One of my men will take her to the hospital and stay with her until we can question her. Evan can you please get in touch with her husband and have him come down here? Don't give him any details."

"Will do." Evan takes out his cell.

Sergeant Phillips stands looking at the Corvette, looks up and says, "Constable Warren, head over to Mrs Oddleifson's and tape off the driveway area. Wait there and secure the space. And send your partner down to M & J's and check out his story."

112

Chapter Twenty — Persons of Interest

Susie peers out the window of the front door. Two RCMP constables walk around the side of the garage. "Now they're poking around the side. Can't see them, damn. What're they doing now? What can they possibly hope to find?" She looks at Steve sipping his coffee. *Does he care?* "Steve. Can you hear me?"

"Honey, come, sit down, eat your toast. They'll find what they find…We have nothing to hide."

"Nothing to hide? We're 'persons of interest' for God's sake! Persons of Interest! Do they think we murdered Larry? Jesus. What's going on? This makes no sense." She paces between the door and front window. Her voice rises, "We have to do something. We can't just frigging sit here drinking coffee and eating toast." *I think I'll go nuts.* "What's the matter with you? Do something! Don't just sit there like nothing's happening for Christ's sake."

Uh-oh, I think I'm seeing Biker Chick Susie. Better do something before she really gets worked up. Steve intercepts her before she reaches the front door again. He hugs her. "Susie, please come and sit down. We'll talk while you eat a little bit. C'mon Honey, this is getting us nowhere."

Susie hugs him back, sobs and says, "I can't take this. We've done nothing. You act as if it's a lot of nothing. It's a nightmare. How can this be happening? You didn't see that little boy. It was awful, just awful." She allows him to lead her to the couch. She sits down and stares at her now cold toast.

Steve says, "Honey, just because I appear calm doesn't mean I am. I'm trying very hard to figure out what on earth's happening…and I'm getting nowhere."

113

"I'm sorry Steve. I'm just scared. This is so evil it's making me crazy. I didn't really mean to yell. Forgive me."

"Of course I forgive you. It's normal. I feel like we're in some kind of nightmare."

Susie nods and says, "You're a mystery writer. You're the expert. What should we be doing? What would one of your characters be doing right now? Would they just sit here doing nothing?"

Steve pauses. "Good question. This is real life, I don't have any control here. These aren't my characters that I can manipulate..." He picks up his coffee and looks off into space. *What would one of my characters do?* "Manipulated, that's how I feel...I feel like I'm being manipulated."

Susie waits for him to continue, then says, "What if you were one of your characters?"

He looks over at Susie. "You know, you're right. If I were writing this, my character wouldn't be sitting here while other people take control, passively waiting. My character, let's call him Arthur, Arthur would be upset of course. But he would be...he would be...What would he be doing?" Steven gets up and starts pacing. "Yes...No...Yes, Arthur would be trying to figure out the connection between everything that's happening. Right!" He stops and looks at Susie. "Right?"

Susie nods, leans forward, waiting.

He sits down. "These crazy things all have to be connected. Let's look at them. The dead animals, the message on the window, dead little Larry...and now his hat, and that tarp..."

"Maybe my biker past is coming back to haunt me. Weezil may be on death row, but the Rumble Riot have a long memory. What if all these things are aimed at me?"

Steve shakes his head. "No. Remember what the message said, 'U R the Bastard!' Not 'U R the Bitch'. I think this is aimed at me. But I've only been here two years. What could I possibly have done to make someone this upset? This is crazy, absolutely crazy…Okay, let's stay on track here. Back to our protagonist, Arthur."

"Okay, what would you do with him right now?"

"Well, it's not what I would do with him, but what would Arthur do. I build a picture of Arthur and then Arthur takes over and does what he wants."

"What do you mean, a picture?"

"Well, what's he like?" He stands and starts pacing again. "I see him as strong, decisive, calm. He's educated and…"

Susie smiles. "And tall and good looking."

Steve chuckles. "Okay, tall and good looking. I can see Arthur being confused by everything that's happening. He also feels helpless. But because he's strong and decisive, and knows he's a bit lost, he comes to the conclusion...that he needs help." Steven turns, excited. "Yes, he needs help, professional help."

Susie clasps her hands together and echoes, "Yes, help."

He stops pacing. He turns to Susie and says, "We need some help, some outside help."

"What kind of help? Evan? He's a former policeman, but he seems as bewildered as we are."

"No, not Evan." He starts pacing again. "He's been great, but we need someone who not only specializes in crime but also the law. Someone outside of all this." Steven turns and says, "Irving!"

Susie's face brightens. "Irving! Of course! He saved me from the Rumble Riot. He's the man."

"We need advice. Irving's the best. And he's at his cottage. We ran into him at Sobey's last week. Let's call him."

Irving sits in the armchair facing Steve who summarizes events and then leans back into the couch beside Susie. She gazes adoringly at her saviour. Irving now sports grey at his temples, but is still a perfect five foot Rob Lowe lookalike, immaculately turned out in beige slacks, a blinding white polo shirt, with a sky blue cardigan thrown casually over his shoulders. The image is complete down to his perfectly shaped bare feet in tan boat shoes. He crosses one wrinkle free knee over the other, sits back and says, "That's one fantastic story, you guys."

Steve and Susie nod.

Steve says, "Irving, we feel like our world has gone crazy. We have no idea why all this is happening. And right now we aren't entirely sure we aren't suspects."

Irving shifts in his chair, opens his briefcase and takes out a yellow legal pad. He closes the case, puts it on his knees and poises his pen. "Let's start at the beginning. Give me every detail, however small."

Steve winds up the account and asks Susie if he has missed anything. Susie shakes her head and Irving clicks the pen closed. "All right, I'm going to go and talk to the police. I want you two to say nothing to nobody. Got that?"

Steven and Susie nod.

Irving stands. "I'll be in touch as soon as I know something. You two sit tight. Call me the minute the police contact you, if they contact you. From now on we're going to be very careful. I'm your legal representative and that's all

116

you tell the police from now on. Remember, no talking to anyone." Irving heads for his car.

Steve and Susie look at each other as he drives off. They embrace and Steve whispers in her ear, "Try to relax now. We have the best help. Irving will find out what's going on, I promise you."

Susie nods, but over Steve's shoulder her frightened eyes stare into space. *I know it's never that simple.*

Irving enters the Gimli RCMP detachment and sighs at the height of the counter. He places his briefcase on the floor and stands on it. The clerk turns, struck silent for a moment. *What a gorgeous man!* She recovers, touches her hair, smiles her brightest smile and says, "May I help you?"

"I would like to speak with the Sergeant. My name is Irving Spellman and I am representing Steven Oddleifson."

"One minute." The clerk leaves, but is back quickly.

"Follow me please."

Irving steps off his case, ignores the astonished look on the clerk's face and follows her down the hallway.

The Detachment Sergeant stands as Irving enters, leans over his desk and offers him his hand. "Sergeant Phillips. How can I help you?"

"Irving Spellman. I'm representing Steven and Susan Oddleifson. Could you bring me up to date on the investigation so far?"

The Sergeant sits back and sighs. "Well, we have a body of an eight year old boy, murdered and staged in the Oddleifson's car trunk and an unidentified tarp and a hat fitting the description of Larry's found in their yard, all waiting on forensics. So that is pretty much the extent of the investigation so far."

117

Irving looks intently at the Sergeant, "There have been some strange events that have occurred at the Oddleifson's home leading up to the discovery of the body. Are these being taken into account in this investigation?"

"Of course. But you have to understand that the Oddleifsons are persons of interest and will continue to be until we have all the facts."

"Understood. Just wanted to make sure that all events were being considered."

"A forensic investigation team from RCMP "D" Division will be arriving to do a detailed investigation. This is procedure in a major crime."

"Understood. Here's my card if you need to reach me."

The Sergeant nods and escorts Irving to the door.

In his car Irving dials the Oddleifsons. "Steve, Irving here."

"We've been waiting for your call."

"Just talked with the Sergeant. They're waiting for forensics and then a team from the city will be taking over. I don't think we'll wait for that. I'm calling Vlad to start our own investigation."

"Good."

"Remember. No talking to anyone. I'll be in touch."

Chapter Twenty-One — Detective Marion Schreiber

Marion Schreiber shifts in her chair, groans and stretches to turn on the printer. It obediently prints the next section: Psychology of Trophy Collection. Pencil poised, she starts reading. A half hour later she looks at her forest of editing marks on the pages and sighs, *God, what crap!* She throws each page in turn at her overflowing waste paper basket. *I'm screwed. Can't write, can't focus, no progress. Gotta get it done. Once the baby's here I won't have time to think, let alone write. Could I be any more uncomfortable?* She rubs her extended stomach. *Shh baby. Mama has to write her thesis. Can't do it with all this kicking.*

She stares at the calendar above her makeshift desk, lingers on the felt penned 'X' seven weeks away, her due date. *What a mess. Maternity leave tacked onto leave to write my thesis. So much for my career plan. Great!...* She pats her belly...*Sorry sweetheart, you weren't planned...Don't you worry, Mommy and Daddy love you. Daddy Douglas, you better make it down this weekend. No excuses this time. Sure, you get to keep going on your career path. Trying not to be a bitch, but really? Here I sit in your family's old cottage with our baby and my writer's block. I can't think of anything but our baby. And I have to pee again. Maybe a walk will help settle you down Baby Douglas and help clear my head. And an ice cream cone would hit the spot. Yeah, an ice cream cone.*

Marion sucks in a breath, pushes on the chair arms, stands and heads for the bathroom. After the chore of sitting down and getting back up, she looks at her reflection as she washes her hands. *Where has that new life glow gone? All I see is brown hair, brown eyes and brown skin. Too brown? I'd better start wearing a hat.* On her way out she puts on her mother-

119

in-law's sun hat, looks in the mirror and smirks. *The height of style.*

Finally ready, she heads out for the seawall. *Another gorgeous day in paradise. One gorgeous day after another, God! Maybe I am a bitch. People would kill for this. Who wouldn't want a few months in a cottage on the lake. Why can't I write?* She reaches the seawall, lumbers up onto it and sets off at a slow steady pace. *Oh, I love walking by the lake like this. And it shortens the walk to town. The lake is so peaceful...I'm learning to love this place. Just wish I could write. What's the matter? Am I bored? Depressed?...guess I could be. Wish I knew more people. But that was the whole point. Not knowing anyone. I could whip up that thesis in no time. Right! How's that working?*

Marion reaches Betel and heads down First Avenue towards the ice cream window at Kris's Fish and Chips. She chooses a double scoop burgundy cherry cone and heads to the beach, licking the sweet pink drips as she walks.

She picks up The Spectator from a bench and sits down. *Nice of someone to leave this. Lucky it's not windy or it'd be all over the beach.* She settles down for a relaxed read. The headline screams: Local Child Murdered. She sits up, her cone forgotten.

A man talking on a cell phone walks by. He sits down on the next bench and continues his conversation. Marion finishes the article and sits back. *Murder!...Here in paradise!...a child!...for God's sake. You don't expect that. Not good when you're called out to a child's murder...but it happens. But here? in Gimli?* She looks around at the idyllic setting. Water gently laps the shore, a pelican dips, touches the surface and gracefully planes to a stop.

*Who would do such a thing? I'm no expert profiler yet, but I bet I could...*on the next bench, the man's voice raises and she glances over.

What's he going on about?...he's strangely familiar. I think I've met him somewhere, tall, very tall, unruly hair, unshaven,

120

clothes look slept in. She goes still, leans to the side and hears bits of conversation.

"…not a damn thing…"

"…oh yeah people are talking but no one is saying anything that would…"

"…respectfully Mr Spellman, I need just one break… Yes…but…"

Marion sits up a little straighter. *Mr Spellman! Maybe Irving Spellman? That guy could be his investigator, Vlasenko I think. He's the one that screwed me on that Sigga Johnson murder. My commendation down the tube. I need a better look.*

She uses the back of the bench to push herself up and walks, licking her cone. She pretends to look at something in the tree over his head and gets a good look at his face. *Yeah, that's Vlasenko. Now how to get his attention? A garbage can…* She walks over and throws in her half eaten cone, turns and starts back.

Vlasenko finishes his conversation and pockets his phone. As Marion walks by she catches his eye, says, "Nice day isn't it."

He nods and smiles. *Another local, another chance.* "It sure is. Is it always this nice?" He looks curiously at Marion's belly and smiles. *Not many days 'till she pops.*

Marion laughs. "I'm not a native, but the months I've been here have been exceptional."

Vlad smiles. "Me neither. Don't live here that is. But you can't help envying people who do."

"I've just been reading about that awful murder. Here in paradise, who would ever believe it?"

Vlad looks at her face. *She looks familiar.* "Pretty grisly for sure. Have we crossed paths somewhere?"

"You look familiar to me too."

"Hmmm, I've been in Gimli before. Maybe we ran into each other."

"Maybe. Are you here on business or pleasure?"

Vlad replies, "Business. You?"

121

Marion laughs. "Well it isn't business, and so far, no pleasure."

"How so?"

Marion hesitates. *Damn. He's good. I'm rusty, giving away too much. At this rate we could be here all day. May as well speed this up.* "I'm on leave from the Winnipeg Police working on my thesis."

Vlad perks up. "Take a seat and tell me about your work. Your thesis, eh? What on?"

Marion carefully lowers herself onto the bench.

Vlad takes a good look at her and remembers, *Sigga Johnson case.* "Now I know where I've seen you. Didn't you work the Sigga Johnson murder?"

Marion smiles and turns. "Yes, I remember seeing you around the station. You're Spellman's investigator, aren't you?"

"Vlad Vlasenko at your service." Vlad extends his hand. "I remember that case. Quite a twist to it."

Marion shakes his hand. "And I'm Marion Schreiber." She frowns. "Yes, the case had quite a twist. Twisted me right out of the commendation I was looking for."

Vlad nods. "Sorry 'bout that. But it all worked out in the end. You got your woman, just not the woman you thought."

She looks sternly at Vlad. "Thanks for the apology, but I'm still smarting from it all. I deserved a commendation. The case was twenty years cold and I solved it. Sigga Johnson hired a guy to kill her husband and she inherited a fortune. I found the guy and got a confession for God's sake."

"And he was charged?"

"He had Alzheimer's...couldn't even be used as a witness. But I got a good enough confession. Then Sigga Johnson appears out of nowhere and we come up here to Gimli to arrest her...Who'd've suspected Susie Campbell had assumed Johnson's identity?...Oh well, the FBI got the Rumble Riot motorcycle gang and you and Spellman got that Campbell

122

woman off scot-free. Win-win-win I guess." Marion feels her anger rising. *My career...this messed with my career!*

Vlad shrugs. "Sorry about the commendation. No hard feelings?"

Calm down Marion...Baby Douglas needs you calm. Marion shakes her head. "So what's your business here?"

Vlad smiles. "Confidential, of course."

"Sure. Couldn't help but overhear Spellman's name when you were talking. What would Spellman be involved in?"

"Who says it's Spellman?"

Marion smiles. "Yeah right. C'mon."

Vlad laughs. "Okay. There haven't been any charges yet, but his client wants his interests protected."

"Oh, the child killing, right? And his client would be?"

"You know I can't tell you that."

"Well according to the paper, someone named Oddleifson is a person of interest. Now that's an unusual name. Seems to me Sigga...I mean Susie Campbell was involved with an Oddleifson."

Vlad smiles and shrugs. "Tell me about this thesis of yours. What're you writing about?"

"C'mon, you're not going to tell me anything?"

"Nope."

Marion sighs. "You'll love my thesis title. Profiling: Mental States Revealed through the Organized/Disorganized Dichotomy found in the Processing of Remains. And I'm getting nowhere fast. That's why I'm sitting here on the beach eating ice cream."

What a gift! I could use her. "Profiling eh? That's something I need right now. I'm getting nowhere fast as well. I'm not having trouble getting people to talk, but no one knows anything."

Yes! I need this, God, I need something real in my life… this could be it! "Seems like we could help each other out. You need my expertise and I need some stimulation and distraction."

Vlad looks at her, mentally weighing the pros and cons. *Nah, Can't do it. Spellman'll kill me.* "No, thanks. I work alone. And I work for a lawyer — you're a cop. If this case went to court we'd most likely be on opposite sides. There'd be a conflict of interest. And from the looks of you, you're in no condition to be investigating anything."

What case? There's no 'case'. "Nothing wrong with my brain. And you said there are no charges yet. If charges are laid, I'll withdraw immediately."

"True, that'd work, but…" *Can I do this?*

"Whatcha gotta lose?"

I'm getting nowhere…I need her. "We'd have to have some ground rules…I'm not being responsible for any pregnant woman, especially a pregnant Winnipeg Police Detective."

"Agreed."

"Everything I tell you has to be strictly confidential."

"Agreed."

"Spellman has to get everything we come up with."

"Okay, but I have to be able to use things in my thesis as a study or whatever."

"Only after the investigation is done...and Spellman has to agree with it."

"That's fine..."

"And you'll listen to ideas from him. He's gonna have ideas."

"With his experience, he can only improve things." *And I need this in my life...things have to improve for me...or I'll go nuts.*

Vlad grins and extends his hand. *God, I hope this works.* "Alright. Let's talk profiling."

Marion leans to the side and shakes his hand. She's startled when Vlad gasps and stands.

"Sorry, leg's acting up." Vlad lets his leg hang loose, shakes it and his knee pops. He grimaces and sits back down.

Marion asks, "What was that?"

"Hockey injury."

"Professional?"

"I was trying out for the Edmonton Oilers. Would've made it too, but this Swede with a million dollar slap shot...well, just say I stopped the shot with my knee...end of career."

"Sorry..."

"Thanks, but let's get down to business."

"Tell me everything you know."

"Okay, Spellman's client is Steve Oddleifson and hold on to your seat. Guess who he's married to?"

"Who?"

"Susie Campbell."

"What? You've got to be kidding. Tell me more."

"The child's body wasn't found simply lying in the car trunk, it was..."

Chapter Twenty-Two — Profiling

Vlad sips his coffee and examines the pictures Marion has taped to the kitchen cupboards. "Nice crime board."

She looks at Vlad and says, "If we're going to work together, you have to share all your information. All of it. You can't just feed me the stuff you think is significant. I shouldn't have to work at getting information — tell it all."

Vlad purses his lips, weighing her comment.

Marion continues, "You know I've talked with Spellman and Boychuk and told them I'm involved. You know they gave me these pics and updated me in a general way, but investigating, and especially profiling uses patterns in the little details. I need you to relax and be open. To help solve this case, I need you to tell me everything, every little detail."

Vlad sighs and says, "Okay, you're right. I've been holding back. But cut me some slack, I'm used to reporting only to Mr Spellman. My not telling you everything starts with the raccoon."

"What did you leave out?"

"I gave you a general description of the posing of the carcass, but left out that the chair it was on had been pulled into the bushes. Boychuk took pictures of the eviscerated carcass and gave them to the RCMP. Another thing I left out was that the legs of the raccoon were held open by sticks in an 'X' behind the body."

"Describe it."

"The sticks were sharpened and stuck into the backs of the paws, then lashed together in an 'X' using some kind of line." Vlad holds up his arms. "Like this…" He scans the photos taped to the cupboard doors, steps over and points at one of

126

the spread eagle raccoon. "You can't see the sticks or the lashing in the pic."

"Okay, thanks. That likely links this with the posing of Larry Musgrove. His hands were hooked into the trunk lid and lifted up when it was opened. Look at the pic of Larry's body, it's repulsive."

Vlad steps to the next cupboard and points at the picture of Larry's body in the car trunk. "Yes, whoever we're looking for is sick."

"Agreed. When the raccoon was discovered, were the RCMP called?"

"No, it wasn't taken very seriously at that time. There were a few foot prints and Boychuk took pics of them... nothing distinctive about them."

Marion takes another sip of her tea, looks at the now cold cup, then says to Vlad, "So what do we learn from the raccoon? The perp is nuts, that's for sure, he, okay it could be a woman, but I'll assume it's a guy, he's expert with a knife — the raccoon corpse was skillfully gutted and cleaned. He likely came in from the beach — it's the most hidden entry. He likely watches the house — the raccoon was put there on purpose, it was posed, and you don't carry around a dead animal in plain sight so it was likely placed in the dead of night."

Vlad nods. "So, definitely nuts, likely a guy, expert with a knife...and? What else?"

Marion looks pensive, then says, "... expert with a knife, so he could be a surgeon, like that theory about Jack the Ripper, or maybe a butcher, or a very experienced hunter. I'm thinking of skinning animals."

Vlad adds, "This isn't a kid. You don't develop this level of expertise in your youth."

Marion shifts in her chair. "Good. And I doubt it's an elderly person. Statistically, a middle-aged person would be more likely. The emotion involved in the Musgrove murder is too raw and the crime's too physical for an elderly person. Older people are subtler, more efficient."

Vlad says, "Another event at the house is the graffiti on the window, 'U R the BASTARD'. Throw in the dead animals on the steps and car hood and I think this whole thing is focused on Steve Oddleifson."

"I agree, if it was Susie, they'd most likely have written BITCH. He's most likely the target. Were the RCMP involved? Did they do any forensics on the writing, the paint used, foot prints? Any photos taken of the graffiti?"

Vlad nods. "They came out and took a pic, only one, but all this wasn't linked or being taken seriously at that point."

Marion shifts in her chair, grimaces and arches her back.

Vlad continues. "Now the kid's murder. Larry's body is staged, but not gutted. Does it appear to be the same person?"

Marion nods. "Larry's corpse and the raccoon remains were posed in a specific pattern. Of real interest is stabbing the corpse and then trying to make it look 'normal' by posing it so it would sit up in the car trunk, like it wasn't dead. This could indicate a devastating event in the perp's past...some event or time that ripped the emotional core out of the perp... and he's been trying to make it all okay ever since. The cross of sticks holding the raccoon's legs open isn't necessarily a religious statement. It could be to display the 'all's okay', everything's fixed now, state of the corpse...or simply that he wants us to see what he's done. Likely he is subconsciously trying to tell us something."

"What do you mean, subconsciously?"

128

"Everything you do is shaped by your subconscious. So, how the perp processes the corpses lets us see into his mind. In a weird way, he's talking to us." Marion looks at her cold tea. "Now, do we think the kid was targeted?"

Vlad stops, thinks a moment, then says, "Interesting thoughts about the perp…Was Larry a target? Hard to say. Obviously the murderer is crazy, but if the perp was targeting Steve, wouldn't he pick someone with more connection or meaning to Steve? Steve didn't even know the kid, so if Steve is targeted, why murder this kid? I'm not so sure. Could be a crime of opportunity, not done with Steve in mind. Who knows?"

Marion says, "I agree. We'll just put a question mark on the item. Okay?" She pauses, then says, "Now, we know the perp watches Steve because he knew that the Corvette was sitting outside M & J Auto. He would have all the access he needs. Anyone living in Gimli is aware that during the week the town is dead quiet at night. He could deposit Larry's body easily. As for any scientific analysis of physical evidence, we need access to the RCMP forensics. What are the chances of that?"

"I'll talk to Spellman and see."

"Okay, the next question is, 'What is the motive?' We think Steve is the target but what is the motive? That we have to work on."

Vlad nods. "Someone has it in for Steve. Someone in his past? Someone here in Gimli? Who has he pissed off to this extent? He hasn't been in town that long, not even two years. Now if it was Susie we could have a field day with suspects. Right on the top of the list would be the Rumble Riot and close behind would be that stepdaughter of Sigga's, Bethany Johnson. She's a piece of work for sure. But it's Steve. I bet

129

it's in the past. We can't rule out the present, but let's start with his past and learn everything we can about him."

Marion looks at Vlad. "Yes, I agree, for sure. Now the third question is, 'Who is the suspect?' We don't have one." She sighs. "I guess we are down to investigating Steve's past and see what we can come up with."

A car door slams and Marion's face lights up. "It's Douglas. He's early."

Vlad is startled at the transformation of Marion's face. *Wow, she's pretty.*

She pulls herself forward using the chair arm and braces with her other arm, she hunches and sucks in a breath. Vlad stands and takes her hand, lifts. Now upright, she waddles to the door.

He watches the reunion outside. They embrace. Douglas' red hair gleams in the sunlight. *He's a ginger. That fair skin must be a bugger to tan. Little shorter than me. Looks pleasant.* Vlad moves away from the door as the couple climbs the steps.

"Vlad this is my husband, Douglas Ryan. Douglas, this is the investigator I told you about, Vlad Vlasenko."

Douglas sets down his suitcase and extends his hand. "Nice meeting you."

Vlad clasps his hand. *Firm grip.* "Good to meet you, finally."

Douglas walks further in and surveys the kitchen. "Good Lord, redecorating?"

Marion laughs. "Almost as good as the evidence boards at work. I used masking tape so don't worry about paint damage."

130

"I'm not really worried…just making fun." He looks at the pictures. *Good God.* "Pretty grisly. I'm worried about you. How involved are you in all this?"

"Douglas…" Marion starts.

Vlad interrupts, "Our agreement is that she's not physically involved. I'm using her profiling skills."

Douglas looks at Vlad and says, "Okay, she's in no condition to be actively involved."

"Hey guys, I'm standing right here. I think I can speak for myself. I know what I can do and what I can't." She turns her back on Vlad and says, "Douglas, you're going to have to trust me."

From behind Marion, Vlad mouths, 'Don't worry'. Douglas nods and says, "I'm sorry, I do trust you. But this is so gross. I mean those photos…I'm worried you'll get involved, really involved. I know you. Once you get an idea in your head, there's no stopping you. It's what makes you a good cop, and it'll make you a great mother."

Marion relaxes and leans into a hug. "I have cold cuts and buns. There's plenty for all of us. Let's eat out on the deck and we can tell you all about what's going on…You two can carry it out. Grab some beer and I'll have water."

After lunch the men lie back in their deck chairs and savour a second beer. A pair of seagulls noisily squabble over the half bun Douglas threw to them on the beach. Marion reviews everything they know about the crimes.

At the end of the recitation Douglas says, "I agree that it definitely seems to be directed at this Steve Oddleifson. How're you going to investigate his past?"

Marion looks at Douglas. "If only we knew a computer whiz…"

"Oh no. Not jeopardizing my job at the police department. Can't do it. Sorry."

"Of course not, Honey. Wouldn't ever ask that. But, you must have a friend. One of your computer friends must be a crime nerd who'd love to be involved."

Douglas looks off into space. "Hmm, Danny might." He turns to Vlad. "Got a buddy who owns his own computer security business. He's always been into police work. Wanted to get into the RCMP, poor guy couldn't pass the physical... He might."

Vlad sits forward. "That would save us all kinds of time. You guys can get into things in minutes that would take us days to track down. We need to know..."

Douglas holds up his hand. "Don't need or want to know. I'll put you in touch with Danny and you can deal one on one with him. Don't want anyone thinking I had anything to do with this. And try to keep Marion out of it too, eh?"

Marion sputters. "I'm not staying out of anything. You can't just..."

Vlad interrupts, "Understood. No one knows Marion is working with me and we'll keep it that way. Thanks a million."

Marion scrunches up her face, starts to say something then stops. *Okay, we'll see about that.*

Chapter Twenty-Three — Pickerel Days

Marion moans softly. "Oh don't stop. That's great! Oh yes. You're the best…Ohhhhh. Oh God." She purrs and pushes into Douglas' hands. "Harder, harder…please, yes. Yes!"

Douglas laughs. "You know what this sounds like, right?"

"Don't care, just don't stop."

Douglas puts both thumbs into the small of her back and pushes gently up and down. He reaches for the oil.

"Oh, don't stop. Please."

"Just getting more oil. Relax now. You're tighter than a drum."

"This isn't tight…last week, my stupid computer just sat there and stared at me. I was beyond tight…I think I went solid…I was desperate, couldn't write a thing. That's when I started profiling for Vlad and it's really been a godsend."

"I get it. But you're still doing work on your thesis, right?"

"Of course, I want that done before the baby comes, but staring at the computer was getting me nowhere. This working with Vlad is only helping."

"Okay, okay, I trust you…What should we do today? Any plans?"

Outside echoes — Bang! "God damn, God damn it." Bang!

Douglas cringes. "What the hell's that?"

Still mellow, Marion murmurs, "That's your neighbour, the oddball fisherman across the road."

Douglas peers through the screen door. "Don't see him."

Marion says, "Oh, he's there. Kinda like a shadow. If you do happen to catch sight of him, he scurries away like a rat.

133

Look into his backyard...he could be a pack rat." She chuckles.

Douglas pauses, sighs, then says, "So, I was wondering, do we have plans today?"

"As a matter of fact, yes. There's a fair of sorts downtown, the first ever Pickerel Days."

"You gotta be kidding, Pickerel Days? What does one do on Pickerel Days?"

"Anything to do with pickerel I guess. Wanna go?"

"Sure, we can drive over and see what's going on."

"Ah, let's walk. Walking is better. There won't be any parking close anyways."

"Let's compromise. We'll drive and park as close as we can and walk the rest of the way. Then we can walk all over the downtown."

"Okay, deal...A little more massage please."

First Avenue at Centre Street is alive. Barricades close off the area. Brightly coloured umbrellas and stall awnings run down one side of the street. The other side is filled with tables, benches, chairs and people.

"The whole town must be out. I smell those mini donuts, let's find them." Marion pulls in one direction but Douglas stops at a sign saying 'Fiskur Ballur' with 'Fish Balls' in small letters underneath.

"Marion, look, they're selling fish balls...haven't had any since my Amma died. C'mon, you're gonna love them."

Marion sighs. "Okay, but donuts next, right?"

They pass a kiosk that sports 'Fiskur Tjörn' in large letters. Children circle the old fashioned fish pond with nets, trying to 'Catch a Pickerel - Win a Prize'.

134

Douglas is delighted. "Look, a fish pond game. I feel like a kid again." Douglas beams as a boy catches a bright red yoyo. "Good catch kid! Neat."

Marion says, "Yes, but I thought you wanted fish balls. And just what is a fish ball? Sounds gross."

"You love fish and you're going to love these. Must be pickerel since it's Pickerel Days. You deep fry a ball of fish! What's not to love? And you can dip it in sauce. I used to only like ketchup, but Amma made a great tartar sauce."

They order ten balls to share. "What kind of sauce do you want?"

Marion looks over the bowls and picks 'honey dill'. Douglas wrinkles his nose. "Can we have two sauces?" The vendor smiles and nods. "Thanks, some tartar please."

They move under a tree and Marion takes her first tentative bite, then puts the whole thing in her mouth and reaches for another.

"Told you so." Douglas smiles. "Now give me a chance." He dips one and pops it in his mouth and mumbles, "Let's find a list of events." Marion nods as she finishes off her third fish ball.

At the dock, they stand hand in hand reading the list of events. They narrow it down to a fish filleting contest at 12:30 and a casting event on the dock at 2:00.

Douglas adds, "And I want to do the Fishing Boat Ride, okay?"

Marion says, "Okay and I want those donuts."

Douglas sighs. "I promise we'll find the donuts. There's time before the fishing boat tour to see the stalls. And after the filleting contest we can squeeze in a bite to eat. I gotta say, the pickerel burgers people are eating look amazing."

135

They walk slowly, admiring the Icelandic sweaters at one booth, the jewelry at another. Douglas buys Marion a polished 'lucky stone' bracelet. She turns it around on her wrist admiring it. "Why are they lucky stones?"

"See those tiny holes in the stones? When we were kids we'd scour the sand for them. We called them 'lucky', don't know why. Maybe 'cause you were lucky enough to find them. I always marvelled at the tiny holes."

"Thanks, Honey, it's beautiful."

Vlad's at the next stall, looking at aerial photos.

"Hi, Vlad. Good to see you." Marion steps towards him.

Vlad's face lights up. "Marion." He looks at Douglas and nods.

"Douglas is going on the fishing boat tour. Want to grab a coffee?"

"Maybe Vlad wants to take the tour, Honey."

Vlad laughs. "No thanks. I like solid ground. No water for me. I'll take the coffee."

Douglas looks at his watch. "How 'bout we meet in an hour at the filleting contest? You can go early and get us good seats. I don't want you standing around too long. Promise?"

Marion nods. "C'mon Vlad, we'll get some takeout coffee and talk." The two detectives settle down on a bench and silently watch the lake.

"God, it's beautiful here. Reminds me of a fishing village on the Black Sea. Used to go there as a kid." Vlad breathes deeply, stretches out his long legs. "I love this. Lake Winnipeg, just like the ocean."

"I know what you mean. I wonder if fishing villages are the same everywhere. When I was in Puerto Vallarta I watched a fisherman seaming his nets and it reminded me of

136

images from other fishing villages — from TV and other trips when I was a kid." Marion laughs. "I used to be a kid too."

Seven pelicans swoop in formation and come in for a landing. "I don't think I've ever seen that before," Marion comments as she savours her coffee. The birds stay together, bobbing slightly on the gentle waves…They sit on the bench, still, quiet.

Finally, Marion brings up their shared business. "So, our killer. I've been thinking. He likes knives, definitely skilled with knives. What type of people would use knives?"

"I've been thinking the same thing. Butchers, chefs, cooks, doctors. Do you think there are still trappers around here?"

"Trappers? That's old style stuff, right?"

"I don't know. But I think we should find out. Why wouldn't there still be trappers? People still want fur, right?"

"First Nation people likely trap for meat as well," Marion adds, "You should ask around for sure."

The two quietly ponder the possibilities. This time Vlad breaks the silence. "In a town this size I find it strange that no one seems to know anything."

Well, maybe you're just not talking to the right people. Who've you been asking?"

"Been going to the coffee shops, chatting up waitresses in restaurants and gas station attendants. I've been to all the bars. I even borrowed a fishing pole and sat at the dock for hours talking to whoever would talk to me. Waste of time."

"Hmmm. Basically what I would have done, except for the fishing." Marion looks at her watch. "Almost time for the filleting contest. Want to come?"

"Sure, why not." Vlad stands and turns around, offers his hand. Marion smiles and accepts his assistance.

137

"Thank you. Being pregnant is not easy."

The two just reach the tent as an excited Douglas runs up. "Now that was excellent. You should have come. It was cool on the lake. It seems so calm on shore but once you're out a bit, it's really choppy…"

"Okay Honey, let's get seats and you can tell me all about it. It's really filling up fast." Marion pulls him along the makeshift aisle and Vlad follows behind. They are just seated when the announcer begins. He reads out the rules and calls the first competitor.

A young man takes his place at the table and from the crowd someone yells encouragement. "You go, Oli. You're the man." He reddens and grabs his first pickerel. His blade gleams. In one motion he slices from behind the gill to the tail, flips the fish and repeats the procedure. Two nearly instant flicks remove the skin from both fillets. He piles the fillets on the scale and grabs another fish.

Eyes wide, Marion turns to Vlad and at the same time they mouth the word, 'fisherman!'

Chapter Twenty-Four — Marion buys a Buffet

Douglas rolls over and reaches out to embrace Marion. He gropes the sheet and pillow, finds nothing. He opens his eyes. *No Marion?* He throws his legs over the side of the bed and sits, scratches his head. "Marion, you making coffee?" No response. "Marion." Still nothing. He sighs and walks slowly out into the living room, looks around. "Marion, where are you?" He peers into the kitchen, out onto the lake deck and finally through the back door. He looks beyond the deck, across the street and down a bit, a speck of colour catches his eye. Marion stands behind a large bush, peering through the foliage. *What in the hell is she doing*?

Douglas slips his feet into his flip flops, walks out, across the yard and down the road. Marion is very still and concentrating. "May I ask what you are doing?"

Marion jumps and turns. White faced, she holds her distended stomach and looks up at her husband. "Shhh. Nothing." Awkwardly she shifts her weight and motions for him to follow her home. "Douglas, you scared me half to death."

Douglas takes a slow breath. "Just what do you think you're doing?"

"Shhh. Wait until we're inside, please."

In the living room, Douglas crosses his arms and says, "Okay, I'm waiting."

Marion walks into the kitchen. "I made coffee. Want some?"

"Sure, coffee, good idea, but I want your explanation as well."

139

Marion returns with two cups, gives him one, sits down and clears her throat. "Well, Vlad and I were talking yesterday about our murderer and thinking that he or she was very good with a knife."

Douglas sits down with his coffee. "So? What has that to do with you spying on our neighbours?"

"I'm getting to that. At the filleting contest we both started to think that our suspect could be a fisherman."

"And?"

"Well, in the night I was thinking about the fisherman down the street. He's certainly an oddball..."

"So you think that the only fisherman you've had contact with is a suspect? Are you nuts? Do you know how many fishermen there are in Gimli?"

Marion squirms. "I know that. But you have to see this guy."

"Marion, be reasonable. He's an oddball, not a murderer! You know that. And, even more important, you're very pregnant. You promised me you're just a resource for this Vlad guy. No field work! What happened to your promise?"

"I know, I know. Sorry. I just got a hunch and wanted to try and catch sight of him...There's just something about him."

"I don't care. This is crazy. You have nothing to go on and you promised me you'd just be profiling, nothing more. Promise me you will leave the leg work to Vlad."

Marion nods.

"No, promise me."

"Okay. I'll leave the leg work to Vlad."

"Good. Now, let's get dressed and go out for breakfast. Then I want to sit on the deck, get some sun and read. It's gonna be a long week."

"Sounds great. I'll cook that pickerel we bought yesterday and we'll have a nice dinner before you leave for Winnipeg."

Marion walks Douglas to the car. "I'm going to miss you. Can you come on Wednesday night?"

"I'll miss you too. I hope I can, but don't know yet. I have to make a date to talk to my buddy Danny about helping you guys, so I'll let you know."

He throws his bag into the back seat and spots the parcel. "Damn. Forgot the package. Honey, would you mind taking this to Mrs Finnson for me? I forgot and Mom'll be pissed."

"Sure. Who's Mrs Finnson?"

"An old school friend of my Grandmother's. She doesn't live far from here, on Third Avenue. Actually, you pass her place every time you walk the seawall. It's the white house, just down from the gray one on the corner."

"Okay, the one with the cute little Pomeranian, right? I think I know the house."

"Yup, that's the one. He's a miserable little shit, so watch him."

"Sure thing. Now, one more hug please."

On Monday afternoon Marion walks slowly along the seawall, *Could it get any hotter, must be the humidity.* She carefully notes each house. Did he say the gray house on the corner or the white house...darn. She pulls out her phone, is about to punch Douglas' number when a series of sharp barks then an angry shout stop her. *Pomeranian!*

She picks up her pace and passes the second house from the corner. In the third yard a tiny elderly woman is tugging on the leash of a snarling dog. "You ungrateful little brat.

141

C'mon. In the house. How many times do I have to tell you that…"

Marion carefully steps off the seawall and calls, "Can I help?"

"Oh, my dear. Georgie is just having a little fit. He'll calm down soon. He's really a sweet little fellow but…"

Sweet little Georgie bares his teeth and snarls at Marion. She hesitates, then asks, "Are you Mrs Finnson?"

She stops, shades her eyes and looks closely. "I am."

"Hello, I'm Marion, Irene Ryan's daughter-in-law. She asked me to deliver this package to you."

"Oh excellent. Come in, have some tea and we'll chat. It's been a while since I've seen Irene. You can tell me all about her travels."

Marion follows her inside staying out of Georgie's striking range. *Charming little place, looks like four rooms.*

"Sit down in the living room and I'll lock Georgie up in the bedroom. C'mon along you naughty boy." She pushes the dog in and closes the door, then heads to the kitchen. "I'll put the kettle on. The last card I got from Irene, they were in Paris."

"They had a great week in Paris. They absolutely raved about it. They're moving on to Greece now. And then I think, coming back via Rome."

"Wonderful! If only I was younger. But, you know." Mrs Finnson laughs. Back in the living room she sets down a tray of tea things and sits with a sigh. "Not as young as I used to be."

The kettle whistles. Marion pulls herself forward using the couch arm, stands and says, "Allow me," and heads into the kitchen.

142

"Oh my dear. I shouldn't. You look like you need some care. How far along are you?"

Marion calls as she pours the kettle, "Seven and a half months."

"Your first?"

"Yes," Marion says, carrying in the teapot. "Before I forget, this is the package."

Mrs Finnson thanks her and places it on the table. "Now tell me all about that lovely husband of yours."

Marion relaxes back into the couch and fills her in on Douglas' career and their plans for their soon-to-arrive baby. The two ladies warm to each other as they sip their tea.

"I love your home. It's darling. You must be very comfortable here."

Mrs Finnson sighs. "I am. I'm going to hate leaving."

"Leave? You're leaving? I'm sorry to hear that."

"I'm moving in with my sister. We can help each other. I have to get rid of all my furniture though. There's no room." She looks around and lovingly touches the table next to her. "Oh well, it's okay. My niece and nephew will handle the yard sale." She laughs. "I guess you would call it a houseful sale."

"You have some lovely things. I especially like that sideboard. It's gorgeous. Look at all that intricate carving."

"It is lovely. You know it came with the house when I bought it. I always wondered about it. I guess there was no one that wanted it. There was a young woman here before me. Tragically, she died right in this room I understand. So young."

Marion's detective senses tingle. "You say she was young? Was she ill?"

Mrs Finnson shakes her head. "No…not ill." She looks around, undecided, then continues. "I guess it can't hurt to tell

143

you. There's no family around anymore, just that poor son of hers. I think there's something wrong with him. But then that's another story altogether."

Marion waits patiently. "What did happen to her? Was she murdered?"

"Oh my, no. That would have been too grisly for me to live here. No, she was so drunk she choked to death. Ruby Gislason was her name. Such a pretty young thing...until she took to drinking of course."

"That is tragic. But that sideboard is gorgeous. Would you sell it to me? If you are selling it of course."

Mrs Finnson's face lights up. "I'd love to do that. How about $100? Is that too much?"

"That would be a great price. I'll bring the money around tomorrow but I can't move it out right away. Douglas is coming on the weekend and we'll come over and we can talk some more. Would that be okay?"

"That would be wonderful. I'd love to see Douglas again. What a nice young man he is."

Marion settles back in the couch and says, "Now tell me all about Douglas' mother when she was a young girl."

Chapter Twenty-Five — Dinner at Irving's

'The Pines' is carved into a time-darkened sign nailed above the door.

Steve says, "This must be the place."

Susie nods. "That's what he told us. It looks very nice doesn't it?" She looks around at the tall pine trees and says, "I really don't know Matlock."

They climb the steps and look for a doorbell. "No button. Do you think we ring this?" Steve points to a decorative iron bell projecting from the panel beside the door.

"Maybe…Can I do it?" Susie smiles and tentatively pulls the cord. They both jump and laugh at the loud clear tone. "What a beautiful sound. I want…"

The door swings open. Startled, they step back. A man, about five foot eight, bald and menacing, barks, "Yeah." A large scar runs from his left eye to his neck. The top of his left ear is missing.

Steve clears his throat. "We're the Oddleifsons. Irving is expecting us."

"Yeah. He's waiting for youse on the back deck." The man steps aside, points towards floor to ceiling windows. Outside on the deck, a figure sits in a chair facing the lake.

Steve and Susie enter the foyer and the menacing man steps around them, leaves and slams the door behind himself.

Dumbstruck, the pair stand still looking at each other. Susie breaks the spell. "What an interesting man."

Steve laughs. "That's an understatement. I think that nose has been broken several times. Did you see the size of his hands?"

"What about that scar that runs down to his neck?"

"What neck?"

Susie laughs. A set of black and white prints over the hall table grabs her attention. "Look Steve, these are gorgeous, it's a young man dancing. Look at his body posture."

Steve takes a quick look, murmurs, "Hmm," and heads towards the deck. "Let's go and find Irving."

Susie follows, looking at everything. Wow, amazing, understated and elegant. She giggles. Just like Irving, perfect. She squints at the writing on the first of five trophies, but Steve motions for her to hurry up. Darn. *Who won all these*? She follows him out the patio door.

Irving stands and walks towards them. His aura of self-confidence gives him stature far beyond his physique. His expected flawless appearance relaxes them. "Susie, Steve, welcome. Oscar must have let you in before he left. So good to see you. Come, come, sit. The lake is gorgeous tonight. I thought we'd have a cocktail out here before dinner."

He hugs Susie and shakes Steve's hand and indicates two comfortable patio chairs facing the lake. "Caesars okay with you?"

"Great," they say in unison. Susie adds, "You have a beautiful place here."

"Thank you. I like it. Inherited from my mother's family. I'll just be a minute."

Irving returns with the drinks, says, "Cheers," and settles down with a sigh. "Now, shall we do the business before or after dinner?"

"Before," Steve says and Susie nods agreement.

"I've had feedback from my investigator, Vlasenko, I think you've met him. He's looking into everything connected with the case, including you Steve." He holds up his hand at the astonished look on his guest's face. "I'll get to that. Vlad's

146

consulting with a profiler and they've concluded that the way Larry Musgrove's body was staged ties it to the raccoon incident, so they feel we're likely dealing with the same person. The body being in your car and the raccoon in your yard strongly links this whole thing to you." He looks up from his drink at Steve. "We don't have any information from RCMP forensics, but Larry's hat and the tarp that were found in your yard will connect everything to you."

Susie sucks in a breath and Steve gapes at Irving.

Irving continues, "The profiler Vlasenko works with sees indicators in the crimes that reveal the way the killer thinks. Of real interest is how the corpses are made to appear 'normal', cleaned up and posed or presented. What's in the criminal's past is very significant and that brings you in, Steve."

"How?"

Irving sits back in his chair. "There's something in your past, or something you've done, or this person thinks you've done that's driving his mind."

Steve and Susie look at each other, stunned.

Irving moves on. "I've asked the RCMP for the formal forensics report, but they won't give me any indication of what preliminary information they've gained. And that's significant."

Both Steve and Susie lower their drinks and look directly at Irving. In unison they ask, "Why?"

"You know you're 'persons of interest' and now they've become very cautious about what they'll reveal to me. I think this indicates their level of 'interest' has increased."

Steve asks, "How? Why're they thinking like this?"

"I think someone has it in for you Steve. You haven't been in town that long, so I think it's in the past, here in Gimli. I think someone's trying to frame you. Ultimately the RCMP will have to put their cards on the table."

"What can I do?"

"Believe me, if the RCMP had anything linking you to the murder you would be charged by now. So, just keep living your lives and please do not talk to anyone about this case. You will not be out of the woods until they find the culprit. Until then, you're their best bet. Sorry. Now, as I mentioned, my investigator Vladimir's in town. I think you two met him when Susie was exonerated."

"Yes, we did briefly," Steve says.

"Well, he's busy digging. He's good. I have total faith in him. He's looking at every angle. The boy's past, and yours too Steve, necessary evil. There has to be something in your past or something you've done that's caused this person to go after you."

"I agree, but for the life of me…"

"Don't lose faith. We'll get there. Now, how about dinner?"

"More pie?" Irving raises his brows and glances from one to the other.

Susie groans, "Saskatoon pie. Was one of the ingredients magic? It was perfect and I'm perfectly stuffed." The men laugh. "Seriously…I've seriously overdone it, but I know why. The rack of lamb really did melt in my mouth and that sauce on the asparagus was addictive. Irving, you're an artist. I need recipes."

"Oh no, not me. But I will tell Oscar how much you liked everything. Glad you liked it."

Shocked, Susie and Steve say in unison, "Oscar?"

Irving looks at them, surprised. "Yes, Oscar. The guy that showed you in. Sorry, didn't I tell you about Oscar?"

Steve shakes his head. "No."

"Well Oscar looks after me. I guess you could call him my personal assistant. He cooks, he cleans, he looks after my clothes and I would be lost without him."

"Oscar cooks!" Susie says incredulously. "That man looks more like a prize fighter turned mobster. C'mon, there has to be a story here."

Steve adds, "Oh please, I couldn't write this."

Irving laughs. "Well I guess it's kind of unorthodox but it just sort of happened. About fifteen years ago I was in a very high profile case and my life was being threatened so I had to hire a body guard. Long story short, found Oscar. He kept me alive and we got along. He's a man of many talents, the least being cooking. I don't pry but he surprises me all the time with little bits of his past. He seems to like the freedom of our arrangement. And I do too, obviously."

Steve says, "Wow, amazing. Like I said, couldn't make this up."

"Well if I ate this way every day I would be enormous. How do you stay so slim? Exercise?" Susie asks.

Irving looks a little uncomfortable. "Well, you could say that."

Intrigued, Susie pushes a little. "What do you mean? You either exercise or you don't."

"Oh, I exercise. Just a little differently from most people."

Steve senses Irving's reluctance and says to Susie, "Honey, maybe it's private. Let's change the subject."

"No, no, it's okay…I tap." Irving waits for the reaction.

"Tap?"

149

"Yes, tap dance. I have for years and years. I was a bit of a celebrity in the dance world when I was a child. And I just kept it up."

Susie eyes light up. "So that's it! Those gorgeous prints in the hall are you, aren't they?"

"Guilty. A local artist did them for my mother years ago."

"And all those trophies, yours too?"

Irving reddens. "Uh, yes. Can't seem to throw them away."

"My God, don't you dare. They're wonderful! Steve isn't this something?"

Steve shakes his head. "Amazing. Who knew! I'm sorry Irving, but don't be surprised if I use this in a book."

"No problem. Just don't use my name, okay?" Irving laughs. "More wine anyone?"

"Yes please," Susie adds, "How about a demonstration and maybe a lesson? We can work off some of this amazing food."

Irving stands. "I'd be delighted. Let's take our wine into the living room. The wood floors in there are perfect."

Irving pushes the coffee table and rug over. "Now, how about a little soft shoe."

The wine bottle is finished and laughter replaces the dark cloud of raccoons, dead bodies and unknown suspects for a little while.

Chapter Twenty-Six — Alexander Plans a Murder

Alexander's eyes glaze over and half close. He tries to concentrate. He snaps the tab off his beer and takes a long swallow. *Okay that slippery bastard is still walking around free. What the hell? Driving his fancy car, smiling and laughing. Why the hell hasn't he been arrested?* He burps. *What do I have to do? Not fair. He has everything.* He guzzles the end of his beer, lets the can roll off his palm and clatter into the pile at his feet. He looks around his room; mismatched furniture, dark smears on the walls. *Nothing, I got nothing!* Ruby screams, ***You're an idiot. You've got nothing. You're an idiot!***

"Shut the fuck up!" He stands and steps through the pile of cans, they tumble and roll as he stumbles to the fridge. "Shut up. Leave me alone."

Ruby laughs. ***What a loser! You'll never have anything. You're no good, you're an idiot!***

Alexander falls into the couch clutching his new beer and it slops onto his shirt. "Now see what you made me do. You stupid bitch! Get outta my head."

No guts, no brains, no gumption.

"Gumption? What the hell? Gumption? I got plenty of gumption. What'ya talking about? I'm smarter and better than anybody. You know nothing."

Right. Sure you are.

"Well I'll show you, you stupid bitch. They'll all pay. I'll make that bastard pay. I'll…" Alexander stops, stares off into space. "I'll…hell, I'll…"

Yeah, you'll what?

151

Anger reddens his face. He sits straight and yells, "Shut up you bitch. I'll make sure he pays. He'll pay big! I'll take something away. Something he loves." He stands and paces around his disordered room. *Something he loves...His car? His house? No...gotta be something they'll put him away for. Put 'im away. Ruin him. He stops, his eyes gleam. Yeah, I gotta kill someone, someone he loves, make sure he gets the blame...Not my Angel Sigga. No, not my Angel. Someone else. Someone else...maybe that bitch Jeannie Baxter, they're close. Yeah, Jeannie. Thinks she's better than me. Asked her to grad, she wouldn't look at me...wouldn't go with me...was a bitch then, still is now. Yeah Jeannie...thinks she's too good for me. Serves the bitch right.*

I gotta be smart about this. Take my time. Work it out. No mistakes. He won't wriggle out of this one. Now how? How to do it? How to pin it on that bastard Steve?

Alexander throws back the rest of his beer, staggers towards the fridge, then sits at the kitchen table. *Okay, gotta plan. Yeah, make a plan. A good plan. No fucking screw-ups this time. I'll watch 'er and figure out the best time to off 'er. Yeah, careful planning this time. No room for mistakes. Now, need a way to pin it on 'im.* He takes a deep breath and feels numbness reach his fingertips. *I guess I'm pretty drunk.* He sits back in the chair and tries to think. His eyes slowly close, but he shakes himself awake. *No sleep, not yet. Gotta finish the plan. Need something to prove that bastard did it.*

Could plant something. Something...what? Needs to be good. No doubts. His head nods. Need something. He sits up suddenly and yells, "The knife, the fucking boy scout knife." He laughs as he stumbles and pulls the cigar box from under the couch. He carries it back to the table, sits and lifts the lid. *My treasures.* He rolls the blue earring in his hand, slips the

152

wedding ring on and off his finger, then grabs the knife and opens its blade. "The boy scout knife! Great. Perfect. I'll kill 'er with the boy scout knife." *This was his.* "Let's see 'im talk his way outta this one." He sits down on the couch and slips the cigar box back under. He fondles the knife. *This is brilliant. I'm telling you mother…brilliant.* His head nods and he falls back on the couch, asleep.

Bright sunlight wakes him. Alexander clutches his head with one hand. *Christ, my head. My fucking head. Water. Need water.* He tries to lift his head off the back of the couch and groans. He lifts his other hand to help and sees the knife. *Wha…*He struggles to clear the fog. *The knife. What the hell?* Clarity slides across his face. *Knife. Jeannie. Finally I'll get that bastard. Made a good plan. But now, water.*

Later, crouched behind a bush in back of the Baxters, Alexander slaps his leg. *What the hell just bit me?* He struggles to write on a pad. *Okay now,* Wednesday, 10:15, garbage. *Jesus, last night it was 10:30. The night before 11:00. Shit! What the hell is biting me?* He rubs the spot through his pant leg. *I can't take much more of this. Damn bugs!* He focuses back on Jeannie. *That pink bathrobe is something else…a little shorter and you could see…*Jeannie bends forward to check something and Alexander leans to catch a better view. "C'mon, a little further…ah damn." Jeannie straightens up and looks around.

    Shit, did I say that out loud? He freezes, *don't breathe.* Jeannie lowers the lid and goes back inside.

    Alexander waits a minute and then cautiously stands and looks around. He slips away down the lane and goes back to his truck two streets over, drives slowly down the street. *Can't draw any attention. Gotta be careful. Let me think. I've been watching that damn house for four nights and garbage time is possible. It's always before midnight. I'll pick a night and just hope for a chance. Ten or later is better, it's dark enough by then. This should be easy. Just pick a night, wait and done!* He pictures Steve being led away in handcuffs and laughs gleefully. *You're done. You're the bastard!*

Chapter Twenty-Seven — Jeannie

"Ernie, let's have a dinner party on Saturday when my sister's here."

"Hmm."

"We can invite the gang. It'll be fun. Like a birthday party for me. How about it?"

"Hmm."

Jeannie looks over at her husband and smiles. "We can get a band and rent the whole Lakeview. Everyone'll love nude dancing and afterwards we'll all go skinny dipping."

"Hmm."

She reaches over and shakes his Free Press. "Ernie have you heard anything I've said to you?"

Ernie focuses and smiles. "Of course dear. Dinner party. Yes."

"Nude dancing, skinny dipping…okay with you?"

Ernie snaps to attention. "What?"

Jeannie throws her head back and laughs. "Joking of course. Seriously, are you okay with a dinner party here on Saturday? Just the gang. It'll be fun while Trisha's here."

"Sorry Honey, Mondays are always busy and this one's a killer. My head's somewhere else. Of course a dinner party sounds great but it's your birthday and you shouldn't be cooking. Why don't we order in Chinese?"

"Sounds great. We do have a very full week. I'll order the birthday cake. Easy! Thanks Honey. Trisha comes in on Thursday and you're picking her up at the airport after your meeting, right?"

"Yes, I won't forget."

155

"And don't forget I have that dinner on Tuesday in the city and I'll be really late."

"No problem, I'll handle everything here."

Jeannie gets up and hugs him. "You're the best. I'm going to get dressed now."

He nods and looks down at his paper.

Jeanie looks back over her shoulder. "Have a good day, dear."

Engrossed in his paper again, Ernie says, "Hmm."

Jeannie laughs and continues down the hallway.

Monday:

10:30 p.m.

Alexander settles in behind the bush and waits.

11:00 p.m.

What the hell? Where's that bitch?

11:30 p.m.

The lights go off in the Baxter house. Sheeit! I guess the bitch took the garbage out early tonight. He sighs and heads back to his truck.

Tuesday:

10:00 p.m.

Alexander crouches behind the bush. Getting a little tired of this. Better be tonight. Someone's gonna see me. I can just see the cops dragging me in as a peeping tom. He laughs to himself. A peeping tom. Right!

10:15 p.m.

The back door opens and Chika dances out. Alexander holds his breath. Jeez, that damn dog. Hope it doesn't smell me. Ernie comes out, locks the door, throws the garbage in the

156

can and whistles for the dog. He snaps on the leash and the pair head down the back lane.

What the hell? Where's the bitch? Now what? Do I wait? He sits for another half hour. Suddenly the lights go out in the house. Christ, he must have gone in the front door. Where's that bitch Jeannie?

Wednesday:
10:00 p.m.

Alexander takes up his position and waits.

10:30 p.m.

Jeannie opens the back door and heads around the corner of the garage to the garbage can. Alexander tenses up and readies the knife. *This is it! Okay, calm now. Steady.*

Jeannie lifts the lid and someone calls out, "Jeannie honey."

Jeannie drops the bag in the can and looks over the fence. "Cindy! Haven't seen you for a while."

"I've been in the city helping my daughter pack for the big move."

"Happy you're back."

"I've been meaning to call and ask about the church rummage sale. Are you accepting clothing?"

"Sorry Cindy, no clothing this time. We'll have a clothing drive in the fall."

"Okay. Good. I'll just keep the clothes for then."

"Remember no furniture or large items, okay?"

"Gotcha." Cindy watches Jeannie lower the lid and head back to the house, then turns around and leaves.

God damn! One more night before the weekend. Can't do it then. Too many damn people walking.

157

Thursday Late Afternoon

The Baxter's front door opens. Trisha bounces into the room and grabs Jeannie. Ernie hangs back, a wine bottle tucked under the arm carrying her suitcase and a pizza box balanced in the other hand as the two sisters rock back and forth hugging and squealing.

Smiling, he says, "Hey c'mon you too. I need a little help here."

The sisters stop and turn towards Ernie. Laughing, Trisha says, "Okay old man, we're coming."

"Here I come bearing wine and dinner and this is the respect I get." Ernie shakes his head as he relinquishes his burdens. "I'm going now. I'll be late, so try not to get too carried away." He watches the two women carry the food into the kitchen talking constantly. *Not much has changed. Still fine looking women.* "Did you hear me? I'm leaving. Got some poker to play. Red, take it easy on the old girl. She isn't as young as she used to be."

Trisha pokes her head out of the kitchen. "Red! How many times do I have to tell you it's auburn?"

Jeannie joins her, patting her brown hair back and posing suggestively, "Who're you calling old? Now scram before you get into any more trouble. Out!"

"I'll walk the dog when I get home," Ernie yells as he heads out to the car.

10:00

Alexander takes up his position.

The mantle clock strikes eleven. Chika gnaws on a crust she found in the discarded box. A nearly empty wine bottle sits on the coffee table. Trisha, curled up in Ernie's chair, looks at her sister and says, "This has been so nice."

Jeannie looks over from the couch. She yawns. "Only the best. We haven't shut up for hours. And I haven't even asked about my babies. How are the twins?"

Trisha says, "Your babies are doing great. Jilly is kicking butt in nursing school and Jody has decided to be a lawyer. Can you imagine? Jody a lawyer? I'm one proud mother."

"And I'm one proud aunt." Jeannie gets a faraway look in her eye. "If only…"

"Ah Sis, you would have made an amazing mom." The sisters look at each other.

Trisha breaks the silence and holds up the wine bottle. "You know I think there're a couple glasses left in this. Let's have a nightcap?"

"Just what the doctor ordered. But let's clean up first and then get in our pjs. I'm on my last leg here."

"I'd love a shower first, okay?"

"Sure, sis. Use our en-suite. We just put in a steam shower, enjoy…It sure is wonderful having you here. We don't see enough of each other."

"Ooh, steam shower. Great. Won't be long."

"I love this bath robe, sis." Trish has a towel wound around her still damp hair and twirls in Jeannie's pink bathrobe.

Jeannie says, "Pink is definitely not your colour but it looks pretty good with your hair hidden."

"Oh, I wear pink all the time, to bed." They both laugh.

Jeannie drains the dishwater. "Okay all done. I'll just run out with the garbage and we can have that drink."

"I'll run that out, Sis. You get into your pjs."

159

"Wonderful. Just make sure the lid is on tight, okay? Darn raccoons just will not leave well enough alone."

Trisha picks up the bag of garbage and opens the back door. Jeannie heads to the bedroom.

Alexander sits up straight, every sense on alert. *Finally. Wait 'til she's at the garbage can. Leave the knife, blame bastard Steve, leave the knife.* He stands very carefully, holding his breath, the Boy Scout knife ready. He looks down at it in his right hand. *Get in shadow. Don't be seen.* He moves tighter against the garage.

Trisha walks down the sidewalk in the brightness of the back door light, then steps into the shade of the garage and stoops in front of the garbage can to pick up a piece of litter. She straightens and reaches for the lid. From behind, Alexander throws one arm around her shoulders pulling her off balance. Stunned, Trisha only has time to say, "Agh…" before the knife slashes into her throat. Blood gushes over Alexander's arm. The garbage bag falls, she lifts her hands towards her neck, but her body goes limp. He relaxes his hold and she slides to the ground. He reaches down and wipes his arm with her bathrobe.

He stands over his kill, his eyes bulge with excitement, adrenaline fires his being. *I feel like God!* He rolls Trisha onto her back, kneels beside her, opens her blood soaked bathrobe and drives the knife into her abdomen. He shifts his grip so he can work the knife down. Just like the raccoon. The back door opens, Jeannie calls, "Trisha, everything okay?"

The words ricochet in his brain, he looks down. *Trisha?! What the hell?…leave the knife…* He steps back into the shadow. *Trisha?* As Jeannie walks down the sidewalk beside the garage, he slips across the lane.

Screaming pierces the darkness. Backdoor lights flash into the lane. Cindy calls out, "Jeannie!"

He slinks away, but the screaming doesn't stop.

Chapter Twenty-Eight — Condolences

Ernie sits mid-couch, barely breathing, looks steadily at the floor between his feet. 'Knock, knock.' Ernie's eyes remain on the floor between his feet. 'Knock, knock.' Ernie lifts his head...dark circles surround his eyes....He sucks in a breath, slowly stands, shuffles over, opens the door and his spirits lift.

"Steve, Susie...Come in. Come in. Good to see you guys." He hugs Steve, takes the casserole from Susie and embraces her with his remaining arm. He leads them to the couch, puts the casserole on the coffee table, sighs and sinks into his chair.

Susie says, "Oh Ernie, we're so sorry...That's a chicken casserole for you two...I just can't believe this has happened." She looks at Steve.

He says, "We came as soon as we heard. We still can't believe it...It can't be true. Not Trisha." He sucks in a breath.

Ernie shakes his head and looks at the floor. "I know. I can't get my head around it. Doesn't seem real. How could this happen? What's going on in Gimli? All that crap with you and now this..."

Susie says, "How's Jeannie? God, she must be devastated."

"She's sedated....She found the body, you know."

Steve exclaims, "No! This is a horror." He moves closer and uncertainly puts his hand on Ernie's shoulder.

Ernie continues, "It's been awful. I pulled into the garage and all I could hear was screaming. Jeannie couldn't stop screaming. Cindy next door helped me get her into the house. The police arrived...called the doctor...everything seemed to

162

happen at once. Still trying to put it all together." Ernie looks blankly into Steve's face.

Susie says, "I'll put this casserole in the fridge and make us some coffee. You sit here and talk to Steve." She lets her hand rest on Ernie's shoulder, then picks up the casserole and heads for the kitchen.

Steve watches her leave. *What in the world can I say? None of this makes any sense.*

The doorbell rings. Ernie leans forward, getting ready to stand, but Susie calls from the kitchen. "I'll get it."

Gratefully, he sinks back again as muffled voices come from the front door.

Ernie says, "Steve, I really don't know what to think here. What's happening? Is there a maniac loose in Gimli?"

Susie walks back to the kitchen with a covered dish. "Another neighbour with food. Coffee coming soon."

"Ernie, what did the police say last night?"

"Not much of anything. They told me about…" The doorbell rings again. Both men watch Susie answer. They both stand as Evan Boychuk comes into the living room.

"Evan, good to see you. Thanks for coming over."

Evan gives Ernie a firm hand shake, pats his shoulder and says, "Sorry, shocked," and sits beside Steve on the couch. An empty silence expands. Evan then asks, "Where's Jeannie? How is she?"

Ernie shakes his head, responds, "She's devastated. The doctor sedated her. Trisha's husband is arriving tonight. Got to pick him up." Ernie sits back and starts to tear up.

Steve offers, "I'll pick him up. Just give me the details."

"Oh God, that'd help. Thanks so much. I have them here somewhere." Ernie rummages through some papers on the coffee table. "Must be on my desk. Just a sec." As if in slow

163

motion he stands and leaves the room. Steve and Evan watch, unsure what to say.

"Evan, she found the body."

"That's ugly…that can't have been good. No wonder she's sedated."

Ernie comes back into the room and hands a sheet of paper to Steve. "His name is Gavin Halbrooke. He's tall…"

Steve says, "That's okay. Met him last year at your BBQ. Don't worry."

Ernie nods and sits again. "Yeah, Jeannie found the body…Trisha is now a body…How?" He sits back and covers his eyes with his hands.

The two men look at him helplessly.

Steve says to Evan, "The cops were here quite late apparently. They taped off the area, barricaded the back lane. They're still out there now."

Evan nods. "Yeah, I tried. Can't get near the area. Did they say anything to you last night, Ernie?"

Susie walks in with the coffee tray. Relieved, the group hands around cups and helps themselves to cream and sugar. Ernie, grateful for the distraction, visibly pulls himself together and tentatively sips his coffee.

"Well," Ernie inhales deeply. "The cops are saying nothing. Last night, when I got home, I could see her throat was cut. So much blood everywhere. You would not believe the blood. Jeannie on the ground beside…" He stops and closes his eyes. *I've got to stop rewinding this scene…get control, I can only help if I have some control…*

After a long pause, Steve says, "It's okay Ernie. You don't have to do this. We understand."

Evan murmurs, "Absolutely. No need."

164

"No. No. I want to do this. Have to make sense of this somehow. It was dark but the yard was lit by the back door light. Trisha was lying on the ground. Jeannie was cradling her head and screaming. Screaming and screaming." He takes a breath. "I felt so helpless. Neighbours came, trying to help. Someone said they'd called the police. Don't know who. I could just see my poor Jeannie and…" He stops and looks at his friends. "Who could do this?"

Steve speaks up, "The same sick bastard that killed little Larry?"

"I don't know. Doesn't seem the same. This bastard slit Trisha's throat…her poor little throat. Musta hit the jugular. All that blood!" Ernie groans. *Control…don't go there again.* He settles in his chair.

After a pause, Evan asks, "Was the body posed at all?"

Ernie breathes in slowly, looks at him. Was the body posed? "Nooo…not at all. Just lying there. Her robe had come open. Her nightgown was soaked in blood." Ernie pauses. *The blood, so clear, how can I tell them…*

Susie looks wide-eyed at Ernie, her mind spins back to the Rumble Riot murder she was forced to watch…*I know how he feels. No, don't go there…* She sits beside Steve.

Steve says, "No posing. Throat cut. Seems more violent. Yes, there are a lot of differences between this and Larry."

Evan nods. "Yeah. But can there be two homicidal maniacs running around Gimli at the same time? Unlikely. But God, it seems like anything is possible these days." He stands up. "Ernie, you need to rest. We'll get out of your way now. If you need anything, just call. Give our love to Jeannie. I mean it, call if you need anything. Anything."

Steve stands as well. "I'll pick up Gavin…If everything's on time I'll be back here around ten thirty…I won't come in,

165

I'll just drop him off…If there's any change, just call, anytime. Let us know about arrangements. And of course, whatever the police come up with."

Evan turns to Ernie. "Let me know if they find a murder weapon."

"Murder weapon. There was a murder weapon." Ernie looks at his friends. "A knife was stuck in Trisha's stomach. Right here in her stomach." He points below his sternum.

"Okay." Evan stops and looks at Steve. Susie hugs Ernie and misses Evan mouthing, "Outside."

At the cars, Evan says to Steve, "Now that's strange. The perp slits Trisha's throat and then sticks her in the stomach. Overkill? Something's weird here. I'm going to see what I can find out."

"Keep me in the loop. God, if this is all connected. I seem to be a target of some sort in this mess."

Chapter Twenty-Nine — Irving's Meeting

Marion stands in the doorway rubbing her back in rhythm with Vlad stepping up her path. "Hi Vlad. Sorry about the smell."

"God, that's awful." A car door slams and Vlad turns around.

Irving and Steve wave to them both. "What's that stink?" they ask in unison.

"Sorry guys. The wind's blowing from the west and it's especially stinky. There's a very messy fisherman across the road." Irving and Steve join them on the deck.

Vlad says, "Mr Spellman, you know Marion from the Sigga Johnson case. Steve Oddliefson, have you met Marion?"

Irving offers his hand and smiles. "Hi again Marion, call me Irving."

Steve says, "I remember seeing you at the police station way back then. Good to meet you. Call me Steve, please."

"Nice to finally meet you as well. Could you guys do me a big favour? I need that sideboard in the house." She points to an antique buffet on the deck. "I was going to refinish it, but think I should get someone to look at it first — tell me if I'd be destroying it."

"Of course."

"Sure can."

Steve grabs one end and Vlad the other and they try to lift it. "Now that's one heavy sideboard."

Irving laughs. "Maybe if you take the drawers out first."

The two men nod, pull them out and stack them.

Irving stops them. "There's something in there." He pulls a manila envelope from the back and hands it to Marion.

Marion, still rubbing her back, turns the envelope over. *'Gislason' in faded red ink.* She holds the door while the two men maneuver the sideboard inside.

Irving looks at his crime scene photos taped to the cupboard doors, smiles. "I see why you wanted us over here for the meeting. Well done." He walks along the display of photographic evidence, nods his head in appreciation.

"Everyone make yourselves comfortable. I made coffee, just help yourself." Marion sinks gratefully into a chair and positions a pillow behind her back.

Steve takes a chair beside Marion. Vlad fills a coffee cup and sits down across from them. A car door slams and Steve says, "I invited Evan Boychuk. I think you all know him. He's been involved with most of the evidence, has been a great help to Susie and me and brings a life of expertise."

Marion takes a breath, tenses, holds the chair arms…then breathes deliberately, slowly, then relaxes. Vlad looks at her… *a contraction?*

Evan gives a short rap on the screen door and seeing everyone inside, enters without waiting for an invitation. "Sorry I'm late."

Irving pulls up chairs, completing the ring around the flokati rug.

Steve clears his throat and says, "Evan, tell everyone a little about your background."

"I'm a retired Homicide Inspector, Winnipeg Police." He nods at Marion, Irving and Vlad. "Think I ran into you all, a time or two." Irving and Vlad smile.

Marion says, "Hi Inspector."

168

Evan looks at her, "Retired now Marion, just call me Evan."

Marion smiles and nods. "We're at my place because I've the hardest time getting around. Why is obvious." She sets the manila envelope on the table beside her. "I met Vlad again on a bench by the beach. I've ended up profiling for the case and that's how I'm involved. I want you to know I'm not here as a member of the police."

Irving responds, "Good, thanks for bringing that up. It could have been a problem."

Steve shifts in his chair, sighs, scans the group and says, "I'm going crazy here and any help anyone can give me is much appreciated. We really have no leads. I don't know why someone has it in for me. And now with this grisly murder..." He begins to tear up.

Irving notices. "Steve, we have five good minds here. We'll figure out how to move ahead." *He's losing his grip.* "Steve, review what we found out from the RCMP yesterday."

He runs his hand through his hair and groans.

Guess it's me. Irving says, "Okay, let me begin. Jeannie Baxter's sister, Patricia was murdered with a knife five nights ago. The RCMP assume the killing is not connected to Larry's murder. There was no posing of the body and the murder weapon, a knife, was found in her abdomen. Although there was a single stab wound in Larry's abdomen, the major differences, the lack of posing and the murder weapon being left, support the current RCMP theory that this is a copycat murder."

Evan leans forward, gaining the group's attention. "I was at Rotary yesterday and had a conversation with a person who has to remain unidentified, but whose information I can vouch for. I was told that the knife was found, inserted to the handle,

169

in Trisha's abdomen just below the sternum. It was an antique Boy Scout knife. This raises a lot of questions that I think are worth exploring, but these facts must not be repeated. They are the kind of detail police use to verify statements and can't be made public."

Steve sits up and listens intently. *Boy Scout knife. My dad had a Boy Scout knife. Had a fleur-de-lis, I lost it, playing with the guys.*

Marion glances at Steve. *That's triggered something. I wonder what?*

Evan continues, "First, the knife itself is an oddity. It's special and may have been chosen for some reason. Next, why leave the knife? She was dead, her throat was cut. Why stab her, especially so deeply and in the stomach? Could the stomachs of Trisha, Larry and the raccoon connect these crimes?"

Vlad looks at Irving who nods. Vlad says, "Yes, we think so. But if that's the case, the last gutting was interrupted. The initial cut in an evisceration can be made below the sternum. I only know farm butchery, but it fits. As I understand the time line, Jeanie Baxter came out within a minute after Trisha had taken out the garbage. She might have interrupted the evisceration."

Irving says, "We really need the autopsy report, and that won't be in our hands for a long time."

Evan leans forward again. "We should focus on the knife."

Vlad says, "As to the knife, Marion and I have done a lot of thinking about the recent events and think a fisherman is a good possibility. Especially given the number of fishermen in the Gimli area and the high level of skill involved in filleting."

170

Marion confirms. "Yes, the perp is obviously highly skilled with a knife. And locally, all fisherman qualify."

Bang…Bang…Bang…echoes outside.

Marion says, "Sorry, that's the smelly neighbour. He usually swears at top volume as well. His yard looks like a five day fish fight and smells like it happened last week. He looks like an ad appealing for donations. I've never gotten too close, but I'm sure he stinks like his place. He sells his fish locally, I think. I've been really sensitive to smells…it's been tough."

Steve looks up. "What's his name?"

"Gislason, Alex Gislason. He's always been over there, as long as the Ryans have been here, apparently."

Steve says, "You know, I remember that name from somewhere, recently..." He looks off, thinking.

Irving says, "Fisherman, that's a good thought, but as you pointed out, there're a lot of people with skill filleting fish. It's a solid thought, but it's only that, a possibility."

Steve thinks out loud. "At the party…someone said..."

Irving looks at Steve, then continues, "We need to lay out some ideas about how we should proceed. What's the next step in narrowing down who could have murdered Larry Musgrove and now Trisha?…Why did Larry's hat turn up under Steve's deck?…Is Trisha's murder done by the same person?"

Steve stares off. "…Gislason…I've heard it recently…"

Irving pauses for a moment. "Who eviscerated the raccoon, put the dead animals on the car hood, the steps? Who wrote on the window?…"

Steve freezes. "The window…the night of the party… Alex Gislason…Jerry Erikson knew him! Damn, he was the

171

fisherman out on the lake. He's always just out there on the lake."

Marion is quiet. *Gislason, she lived in that house...Damn, she originally owned the sideboard! Yes, Ruby Gislason.* She looks at 'Gislason' written in red on the manila envelope and rips it open.

"My God! Gislason! The sideboard." Her face contorts with pain and she gasps.

Startled, the men look at her, concerned, bewildered.

She blows out a breath while reading one sheet after another, looks at Steve and tries to speak... "Look." She holds it up. "The sideboard. Here's a deed for the house where I bought the sideboard." She passes it over to Vlad.

Vlad reads, "Oddleifson, Richard Oddleifson. The house belonged to Richard Oddleifson. That could mean anything, but it's quite a coincidence."

"Richard Oddleifson! That's my Dad!" Steve turns towards Vlad, stunned.

Marion shakes her head, relaxes as the pain passes. "Wow! Look at this! A birth certificate! Alexander Gislason, son of Ruby Gislason and Richard Oddleifson."

Steve grabs the certificate. "What the...my father? This can't be right. Has to be someone else."

Irving takes the paper from him. "Steve how many Oddleifsons do you know who aren't related to you? It's a pretty unusual name, even for Gimli."

Steve shakes his head. Marion and Vlad look at each other, amazed. Irving keeps reading. "There's an agreement here as well. Between Richard and Ruby, all about disclosure...I need time with this."

Marion nods. "This could be important. Ruby Gislason died in the house where I bought the sideboard. She choked

172

and died in that very room. I wonder how old her son was then?"

Vlad cocks his head, thinking.

Steve stands and says, "I have a brother? And my father was… that's it! It's him. Alex is a bastard, a real one. He really is a bastard! But the window said 'U R the bastard'. He was trying to say that it's me, I am the bastard, not him."

Steve paces back and forth thinking…suddenly he turns around, then runs at the door, yelling, "It's him. It's all him. I'm going to…" He tears out, running upwind, towards the rotten fish smell.

Boychuk says, "Shit," and pulls out his phone…"Hello, Sergeant Phillips, emergency…No, interrupt him…Sergeant, Evan Boychuk here. There's likely a major crime about to happen outside the Ryan cottage in South Beach on the lake… Send a car immediately. That's right…quick as you can." He runs out the door after Steve.

Marion, Vlad and Irving sit, stunned. Marion grabs the arms on her chair. "Oh…oh…" She pulls herself forward and strains to stand. Irving and Vlad both stand to help. "Oh My God…" Her hands grab the chair arms and she leans forward. Her water pours down her legs into the flokati rug.

Irving steps back, eyes wide, mouth agape. His eyelids flutter and roll back. He falls to the floor, his phone clatters under the table. Vlad steps in front of Marion, takes her hands firmly, looks into her startled eyes and says, "I'll help you lie down here on the rug. Stay calm."

Chapter Thirty — My Angel Sigga

Susie pulls onto Highway 9 and accelerates to highway speed. *Still quarter of an hour 'til the Emporium's open. Love their stuff...I'll get something nice for Steve. God he needs cheering up, or some distraction...he sure needs something... maybe that figurine for his desk, yeah...and a cup of their tea for me. What the heck, I need cheering up too. Think I'll get one of their sweet crêpes.*

Alexander's foot is about to land on the first step of G & C Grocery and a teen pushes past him. *Damn kids.* At the counter he asks for a coffee and the proprietor Sam, on the phone, points to the pot. Alexander pours the steaming coffee into his cup and tolerates the one-sided conversation. "Yes... No, you can't...Doesn't matter...you're on the list, it's you, you gotta go...so, that's it...Well you're finished here." He jerks his head back from the receiver, slams it down and stares off into space and mutters, "Damn, now what the hell do I do." He looks at Alex, looks him up and down. *Pretty scary but hopefully clean.* Unsure, he cautiously says, "Hey, you wanna make fifteen bucks?"

Suspicious, Alex asks, "Doing what?"

"I got ten pizzas that need to go to the Winnipeg Beach Curling Club...some sorta meeting."

"Well..." Alexander hesitates.

Desperate, Harry says, "Twenty bucks and keep any tip you get. And if you do good, you could get more work."

"Messes with my day, but, okay."

174

A pile of boxes land on the counter in front of Alexander. He's startled and laughs. Harry says, "They've paid for them. They get a two litre with each, so take ten. Use those boxes."

Alexander asks, "Whatcha talking about?"

"Put ten two litre bottles of pop in a couple'a those boxes. It's included in the order."

"What kind?"

"Just take a variety."

Alexander sighs and roots around in the cooler. Outside, he secures the pile of boxes in his cargo bed and gets in his truck.

At the Emporium, Susie's tea's beginning to cool, but Mary, the only person working behind the counter, arrives with a hot pot. "Looks like it needs refreshing. My break time, okay if I join you?"

"Please, Mary, that'd be great. So who's working the till?"

"You're looking at her. We aren't busy."

"Thanks for the gift wrapping. My husband'll love it."

"You're more than welcome, I like those mini sculptures. You'd think it was a man doing it, working in metal like that. To me they look very masculine, but made by a woman."

"Really? I would have thought a man as well."

"That one's been on sale a long time. Why that one?"

"Steve's an author, it's for his desk."

Clearly impressed, Mary says, "Really!"

Susie checks her watch. "Hate to leave, but I've got to get back. It's 1:30, I've been here over an hour."

"Say 'Hi' to Steve. I hope he likes his new desk companion."

"I'm sure he will."

Susie drives north out of Winnipeg Beach. A truck facing

175

south is stopped, sticking a bit too far into the road, like it didn't quite completely pulling over. Susie slows and gives the truck a wide birth. In her rear view, she sees legs sticking out from under the ditch side of the truck. *Wonder if there's trouble?...better check...*She pulls over and backs up.

She leaves her door open and walks around to the ditch side of the truck to see if she can help. *I've seen this truck around Gimli, a local...*"Hello, do you need help?"

From under the truck a gruff cough is followed by, "No, it's fixed. I'm okay." The legs waggle back and forth as he works his way out.

Alexander sits up and looks at his rescuer. Astonished, his face lights up.

My Angel...it's my Angel... "Sigga!" He stands. "I dream about you and here you are." *She's here, my Angel...*He shakes himself and moves towards her. "You look beautiful today. I like your hair. Your jacket is blue, my favourite..."

Susie steps back, thinking, *What? Is he nuts?* He steps towards her slowly lifting his arms, seeming to prepare for a hug. *I'm outta here...*She turns and runs for her car.

Three large steps and Alexander grabs her shoulder, stopping her at the car door. Susie gasps and swings her purse. It glances off his neck and he shakes her. The purse falls to the road. She grabs the door post and wriggles from his grasp. His next hold is firm. She winces at the pressure on her upper arm. He twists and drags her towards the truck.

He murmurs, "My Angel, My Angel," over and over.

Susie screams, "Help! Help! Help!"

He opens the door with his free hand and throws her over into the passenger seat. He climbs in and thinks, *Gotta shut her up, keep her still...fear, she's gotta be scared enough...* Susie lashes out, yelling, help, help. She slaps his cheek and

176

tries to push him away. He reaches over and grabs her throat, squeezes and screams into her face, "You're mine, you're my Angel, you're mine…"

Susie's face contorts, she can't breathe…her thoughts reel, back, back…the Rumble Riot passing her around the gang… s*urvive, live, breathe, stay alive…the pain, the hits, rape, fear*…bile rises in her throat, she chokes. Her eyes roll back and she passes out. He loosens his hold as she goes limp.

Oh no, God, I've killed my Angel…just like little Larry… How?…Disgusted, he throws her against the door, the back of her head whacks the window and she crumples to the floor. *She's dead. Now what? What…*

He starts his truck and does a 'U' turn. *Gotta think this out…Gotta get away from here…where to go, where to go…* He steps on it. His eyes scan the speedometer. *Whoa, 120kph don't get stopped, not now…*He slows to the limit.

Where to go, need to think…

Ruby starts screaming in his head. ***What an idiot…killed your true love, you're a loser, a total loser, you're no good… no good…no good…no good loser.***

Alexander drives north towards Gimli, slows and stops by the bridge at Willow Creek. He puts his arms on the steering wheel, lays his head down, sobs and says, as if to his mother, "She's dead, my Angel, dead. I killed her. I'm an idiot…a real idiot. What the hell happens now?" ***Done, now you're done, a loser that's done…HaHaHa…loser, loser.***

He sits up straight and shouts, *"Mother shut up!"*

Susie moans, sucks in a breath. Alexander gasps and leans over her now hunched body. *My God…she's alive. I'm okay. Everything's okay.* ***You're never okay, you're a loser, a loser, you're no good, no good.***

Home, I'll take her to my place, we'll figure it out there.

177

Conscious now, Susie keeps her eyes tightly shut. *Play for time. Think, Susie, think. He's obviously nuts. He thinks I'm Sigga. I better just stay unconscious. Make a plan. I've been in tight situations before. Just have to stay alive. Do whatever I have to do.*

Alexander looks at her. *Thank God she's breathing. I'll just get her home and then figure what comes next.* He pulls onto South Colonization Road. *Home, just around the corner.* He drives onto the street that crosses his road. *Cop car! At my place!* He passes the end of his road, drives back onto Seventh Street. *Gotta get lost. They're on to me...They can't have my Sigga...Where can we go?*

Ruby starts yelling again, ***Back to where it began. The old homestead shack, where you started life.***

"Mother...that's a first, you helping me...and with a good idea...we'll head for where I was conceived...out Burma Road, back to the start of it all."

Susie tries not to shiver, *Oh my God, now he's talking to his mother.*

The truck roars out of town, west on 231 then right onto Burma Road. Susie huddles in silent terror, thinking, *Okay, he's beyond reason. Nuts, completely self-absorbed. Where's he going? He's looking for something, searching.* Suddenly he lets out a grunt and turns the truck into the bush. Branches brush the doors, scrape against the windows. Then the trail widens. Slow, rough progress ends in front of a small dilapidated house. *Where the hell are we?*

Alexander opens her door and picks her up. He croons, "You're mine. We're gonna live here. Our house. We'll be happy here. You'll see." He walks through the waist deep grass. Susie can feel the tall stocks brushing against her. He

178

hesitates in front of the stoop, then steps gingerly onto the lowest stair, it creaks but holds their combined weight. The door opens easily and out of the corner of her eye Susie sees a kitchen counter at the far end, the furniture consists of a bed, a broken couch and an easy chair with the stuffing poking out. He lays her on the bed, grabs twine from the kitchen counter, pulls her arms through the metal bedhead and ties them together.

Susie thinks, *I'm tied up, but so far alive. What's he want? What's his name? Think Susie, you've been in tougher spots, think. We're miles from anything, He hasn't gagged me, so keep quiet.*

Alexander walks outside. *Gotta check this place out. I've got a few days, food. Hope she likes pizza. There's gotta be water here somewhere. There's the outhouse.* He walks a circuit around the house and finds a well with an ancient pump without a handle, a shed filled with old pails, rope and tools. *Everything I need.*

He re-enters the shack and looks at his still Angel on the bed. He approaches and stands gazing lovingly down at her. *My Sigga's so beautiful. I hope she wakes up soon. What if she doesn't wake up? …Of course she'll wake up…She has to wake up.* He turns and walks over to the easy chair and sits down. *Now I guess I just wait. She'll wake up soon. I have food.* He jumps up and leaves the shack.

Susie cautiously opens her eyes and looks around. *A table and chair under one of the windows…looks like it hasn't been opened in years. I could break it.* She looks for something heavy to use and spies a large iron doorstop by the wall near the door. *Good, that'd work, if I get a chance. Need him to fall asleep or somehow drive off. I must be dreaming, he'll never*

179

drive away. Okay. What else? She tries to reach the knots above her head, but with no luck. *Somehow I have to get him to untie them. I'm going to have to make friends with him. I wonder just how crazy he is. I'll have to watch him for a while. That means I have to wake up. Not many options.*

The door opens and she shuts her eyes. Alex enters with a two litre coke, a couple of boxes of pizza and an old sleeping bag over one shoulder. He deposits everything on the counter and approaches the bed. *Still out.* He covers Susie with the sleeping bag and sits back down on the chair. He sighs. *It's going to be a long night.*

Chapter Thirty-One — Blood, Birth and Chaos

Dazed, Marion looks at Vlad. "What's happening? Is this it?"

"It's started but we have time. Trust me. I've assisted at many births. I know what I'm doing."

She relaxes. He leads her to a dry section of the rug and helps her lie down. He props her back with three huge couch cushions. "My mother was a midwife. I helped her." *Okay it was once and the rest of the births were cows — what is, is…*

Marion opens her eyes, wide, grabs one of the cushions, sucks in her breath and yells, "Oh…Oh my God…"

Vlad says, "Excellent. Breathe. Breathe." He looks at his wristwatch.

Marion relaxes as the contraction subsides. "Oh my God, that was a humdinger. Do you think they'll get here soon?" She breathes deeply, calming herself. "Okay baby, take it easy now." She rubs her stomach. "Hold on 'til we get to the hospital. No rush now…Vlad, what's next?"

"Hospital is next. They'll look after everything. No worries."

"Okay…This isn't supposed to happen for a few weeks… Can't believe it…It's too early…I'm nowhere near finishing my thesis…This could be one of those false alarms."

"No, I'm pretty sure once the water breaks it's time for the baby to come."

"It's gotta be a false alarm…"

Irving's head rolls slowly to the side.

"What about him, he okay…"

"Yeah he's okay. Now just relax. We should have lots of time here. Are you comfortable? Want some water?"

Marion shakes her head. "No, no water. Just want the ambulance to get here. What's taking them so long? Her body stiffens, she grabs Vlad's hand and moans. He grimaces as Marion squeezes. Vlad thinks, *This contraction's too soon. Where's the ambulance?* He looks towards the door, realizes, *Damn...Boychuk didn't call an ambulance. He called the cops!*

Marion's eyes open wide. "Ahhhhh...ghghgh... OOOOOOO...ohooooh."

Vlad's voice fades into the bathroom as he runs to grab towels. "Okay, no problem, hold on. We've got this. No worries. Don't push, don't push."

Marion sucks in a breath, screams, "For God's sake, where are you? Don't leave me now! Son of a bitch!"

Vlad returns, kneels and shoves towels under her legs as far as he can without lifting her. "Don't push."

"I'm not pushing, you idiot. Something's happening!"

Vlad lifts her skirt and groans. "Yes, okay, hold on. Hold everything. I've got it." With his fingertips he gently urges the baby's head. Marion's hips rock and it slides onto his hand. *Relief. Wow...* Her body relaxes back onto the cushions. Her skirt falls as she moves back. Remembering his mother, he rolls the baby over in his hand and softly rubs its back with the pad of his finger. It struggles, not breathing. Vlad rolls it onto its back and blows gently onto its face, then rolls it over again. A hesitant breath. Vlad smiles. The baby takes another, and another...

Irving moans and half sits up, looks at the baby, slick with amniotic fluid and streaks of blood. His eyes roll up and he slumps back onto the floor.

"Marion, you have a boy. A little boy." Vlad cradles the child and tears fill his eyes. "A little baby." The cord pulls at

182

her skirt as he swaddles the newborn in a towel and places it on her chest.

The door slams open. Guns drawn, two constables burst in. "Police! Freeze!"

Vlad yells, "For God's sake, put the guns down. It's a baby. We need help. Call an ambulance."

The constable stops. *What the hell?* His eyes adjust to the light. He holsters his pistol and looks at his partner who closes the door.

Marion brings her arms up around her baby, looks down into the very new, wrinkled face and smiles. She touches the tiny nose. "Hello, little one."

The constables walk over and gaze down at the pair. One takes out his phone. "Hello…Ambulance needed, birth in progress, no, wait, baby here." He gives the address then pockets his phone, says, "I'll move the car for the ambulance," and steps outside.

Irving sits up again and tries to focus.

The remaining officer picks up an afghan and covers Marion and the baby.

Irving props himself up and looks over at Marion. "Whaat happened?"

Vlad smiles, "We have a baby boy."

A dazed Irving repeats, "It's a boy?"

The officer helps him onto the couch.

The first officer returns and they both stand, gazing, awestruck.

In less than two minutes, the ambulance tires crunch on the driveway gravel. The door opens and two attendants wheel in their gurney. Vlad explains, "The cord hasn't been cut and the afterbirth hasn't arrived." They lower the gurney beside Marion and eight hands slip under her. The warmest red blanket in the world is rolled out on top of the pair and she smiles at everyone. Vlad exhales, relieved.

One constable opens the door and the other marches behind as the two paramedics whisk Marion and child out to the ambulance. In moments, they're gone, the police car leading.

Vlad sits down beside Irving on the couch, takes a deep breath and says, "Now, where were we?"

Irving rolls his head and looks at Vlad, mouth open. He slurs, "Oh my God. That was awful…I mean amazing. Sorry, I was useless." He frowns, paws at a stain on his sleeve.

"Where's your phone? The police went with the ambulance. We still need them over at the fisherman's. Steve and Evan haven't come back. Can you get up?"

Irving feels in his cardigan pocket for his phone, sees it on the floor under the table and points. Vlad picks it up, says, "I need a moment. You call the cops," and hands it to Irving who shakes his head, blinks a few times, then presses the RCMP speed dial. "Hello, we called for assistance concerning a…" The door opens and Douglas walks in, pales at the mess on the floor and says, "What's going on?"

Irving continues talking to the police.

Vlad stands and walks over to Douglas. "Congratulations Dad, you have a baby boy!"

"What? It's too early. Way too early."

"No matter. Go on. Get to the hospital. Mom and baby just left in an ambulance."

Douglas looks startled. "Ambulance? Is she okay? Is she okay?"

"She's fine, and the baby's fine. Go." Douglas runs out the door.

184

Irving disconnects and says, "RCMP coming right away. Let's get over and see what Steve and Evan are up to."

"We don't know where this place is."

"We'll just follow the smell."

Vlad helps Irving stand and the door opens.

Evan walks in. "What happened with the RCMP? Why the ambulance?" He scans the scene. "What more can happen? Boy or girl?"

The household phone rings. Irving looks at his cell. Evan picks up the phone. "Hello…No, Douglas isn't here…Yes, this is the Ryan place, but he's not here…Urgent? I'm Evan Boychuk, I'm involved in the case…Okay Danny…Yes…One moment."

Vlad and Irving are at the door, waiting. Evan says, "Are the RCMP coming back?" Irving nods. "I left Steve at Alex's shack. It looks like a possible crime scene. I'm worried he'll go inside and mess it up. This is Danny on the phone with info about the case. I'll take this call. Could you two go over and be with Steve?"

Irving nods, Vlad says, "See you over there."

Steve turns as the two men walk into Alexander's rundown home. He looks back at a cigar box open on the table in front of him. "He's not here. Alex's not here."

Irving walks over and places his hand on Steve's shoulder. "You know this is breaking and entering? What's all this?"

Steve shakes his head. "Not breaking and entering if the door's open. Right?"

"And this box, was it open too?"

"No. I found it when I was looking for clues, clues, anything that will tell me who this person is…Look at this stuff. Most of it's mine. My stuff. Here in this mess. Some of

185

it is my stuff...look, my 'Catcher in the Rye'. I caught hell for losing that. And see my..."

Irving stops him. "Steve, the police are on their way. Let's wait for them outside."

Vlad urges Steve towards the door. "You need some air."

Steve laughs, almost in tears. "Air? Have you smelled this dump? There's no air here."

The two men usher Steve out onto the road as the RCMP pull up.

Irving introduces himself and starts to update the police. The constable interrupts, "Is one of you Steve Oddleifson?"

Steve says, "Yes officer, I am."

"Mr Oddleifson, I am sorry to report that your wife's car has been found south of town, door open, purse on the road. No sign of your wife. Would you mind coming down to the station. We need help ascertaining your wife's whereabouts today."

Steve turns white and crumples. Vlad catches him before his head hits the road. The four men put him in the back seat of the patrol car. Irving says, "I'm his lawyer." And he climbs in beside Steve without waiting for an invitation.

The RCMP constables drive away with them in the back seat.

Vlad turns towards his car as Evan walks up. "I got serious news from Danny. He couldn't get into the RCMP data, but talked with an inside 'friend'. The DNA blood work has been completed. The boy scout knife was the murder weapon in another murder."

Vlad nods. "Larry."

Evan replies, "No. You're never going to believe this one. Richard Oddleifson!"

186

Chapter Thirty-Two — The Knife

A tall, middle-aged officer in RCMP blue serge approaches Irving at the detachment counter. "I believe we've met. Irving Spellman isn't it? The lawyer in the Johnson case a few years ago."

Irving glances at the crown on the epaulet and shakes the offered hand. "Yes, I remember you, but sorry, I've lost your name."

"Inspector Williams, out of 'D' Division. I've been assigned to this case as the lead."

"I'm representing Steve Oddleifson's interests."

Inspector Williams turns to Steve, "We need to sit down and talk. Let's go to the interview room." He looks at Phillips. "I assume it's available, Sergeant?"

"Yes, all set up." The sergeant leads the group into the back of the detachment building.

Williams asks Steve, "We have several things that we've got to go over. Are you feeling up to answering a few questions?" Steve nods as they walk down the hall.

Steve, stricken, sinks into an empty chair. "Where's Susie? What do you know? Where do we start?"

Williams nods at Sergeant Phillips to take the lead. "Her car was found at the side of the highway south of town with the door open and her purse on the shoulder. We need to go over where she's been and what you know about her plans. Why was she out on the highway? Do you know what her plans were for today?"

Steve visibly pulls himself together. "Well, I had a meeting to be at, but she left before I did. I know she was going to the

Winnipeg Beach area for something. Where could she be now? What the hell's happening?"

"The officers found her car at about one fifty…" He checks his watch. "just two hours ago. The tires were cold but the engine block was still warm. Tires cool quickly, but the block would take hours to cool right down, even after a short drive. So it was likely around one thirty that she disappeared. Her car was on the right hand side going north, so it appears she was returning from Winnipeg Beach. Do you know why she was going there?"

"Not really. Oh God, I only half listened to her. Why didn't I listen…I only know she said Winnipeg Beach. I don't know where she was going or if anyone was expecting her." Tearing up, he looks from face to face.

Irving reaches over, squeezes his shoulder and quietly says, "It's okay. Let's get these questions over with."

Phillips continues. "That's good, you knew she was going to Winnipeg Beach. What were you talking about just before she left? What do you think she could have been going for?"

"We really didn't talk about that. Just, I'm doing this, you're doing that. That's it. I was distracted. Not paying attention. God, I'm so sorry. If I'd only listened…"

A constable enters with an evidence bag containing the cigar box from Alexander's and places it in the middle of the table. Inspector Williams clears his throat and Phillips leans back in his chair. The inspector says, "We've retrieved this box of items from the Gislason house." The constable puts on latex gloves, removes the box from the bag, carefully lifts the lid and pulls out the cover of a book. Irving watches carefully. The inspector continues, "We haven't had much time with this box of items, but your signature is on this book cover. Do you have any idea how that could be?"

188

Irving interrupts, "And how is this connected to Mrs Oddleifson's disappearance?"

"We're looking for background."

"I need to consult with my client."

Steve glances sharply at Irving, shakes his head and says, "I want to do anything I can to find Susie." He turns back to Williams. "That's the cover off my Catcher in the Rye. I caught hell for losing that, must have been grade eleven…or twelve. There are other things in there too that are mine…" Irving leans closer to Steve and touches his arm to stop him.

Williams, catching this last statement, asks, "Have you seen this box before?"

"Yes, I looked through it."

"When did you look through it?"

Irving applies more pressure to Steve's arm and quietly says, "Stop."

He leans forward to make eye contact but Steve continues, "I found it this afternoon. Hadn't seen it before that. Most of the stuff in the box's mine, or it was once, long ago." Agitated, Steve looks from the inspector to the sergeant, then sucks in a breath and asks, "Susie's missing. How does this have any bearing? None of this has anything to do with Susie."

"Why were you in Mr Gislason's house?"

"I just found out he's my half-brother today, from that bureau, the birth certificate. You know."

"No, actually we didn't know about that. Could you tell us more?"

"It looks like Alexander Gislason's my half-brother. Our father is Richard Oddleifson. We're half-brothers. Just found that birth certificate at Marion's. None of this makes sense to …"

Irving takes in a breath, about to object, but the inspector clears his throat and looks steadily at him. "I know the stuff in the box doesn't look connected with Mrs Oddleifson, but we need all the background we can get." He shifts his view back to Steve and asks, "Your initials are carved into this, looks like the toe cap from a runner. Is this from one of your runners?" The constable holds it up.

Irving tries to get Steve's attention, opens his mouth to speak, but Steve responds, "Yeah, like I said, most of the stuff..."

"So, when did that pair of runners disappear?"

"I don't know, maybe grade six..."

Irving says, "I'd like to talk with my client."

"Go ahead," responds the Inspector.

"In private."

"Shortly. If you could just bear with us, we think this box is pertinent to Susie's disappearance."

Irving tries to object, "I have to insist..."

Steve interrupts, "No, I want to help. Whatever it takes."

Sergeant Phillips gets up and leaves the room.

The inspector continues, "There's a ring as well." The constable holds it in his palm.

Steve says, "I don't recognize that. I never had anything like that."

"It's likely a man's wedding ring. That mean anything?"

Irving squeezes Steve's arm, forcing his attention. "Mr Oddleifson, as your lawyer, I advise you to stop."

Steve looks at Irving and pleads, "Look, we have to do whatever it takes to find Susie." He turns back and answers Williams, "My father was murdered when I was in grade twelve. His wedding ring was never found. It's the only thing

190

I thought to ask for at the time…the murderer was never caught. Could this be his ring?" Steve sighs and sits back.

Irving looks into the inspector's face and says, "These questions are not related to finding Mrs Oddleifson. Mr Oddleifson has had a very full, trying day. I'd like to continue tomorrow."

"Just a few more things if you can spare a couple minutes Mr Oddleifson." Steve nods. Irving rolls his eyes, exasperated.

"Does this have any meaning for you?" The constable holds a blue earring in his palm. Steve looks at it and shakes his head.

Sergeant Phillips returns to the room with another evidence bag that he lays in front of Steve. The item is hard to see through the plastic, so the Sergeant presses around it, making the fleur-de-lis clear. Steve stands, his eyes bug. "That's my dad's knife!"

Irving takes a deep breath, stands and takes hold of Steve's arm. "Mr Oddleifson, I must insist on talking to you in private, now."

Steve exclaims, "But it is! I'd know it anywhere. I got hell for losing it."

The sergeant asks, "How was it lost?"

"I was playing in the woods with my buddies and it disappeared, just disappeared."

"When was that?"

"I was in grade six, the summer after grade six."

"We will need the names of your friends."

"Sure, Benny Olson still lives here but Ralph Waters was air force and we lost touch." Steve looks helplessly at Irving. "I don't get any of this."

191

Irving, still standing, says, "I am stopping this interview now. We are leaving now Steve."

Bewildered, Steve looks into Irving's tight, concerned face and sighs. "But…" He looks at the officers. "I want to help. Please look for Susie. Tell me what I can do. My friend Benny…" Irving holds the door open and Steve reluctantly leaves.

Sergeant Phillips looks at Inspector Williams and says, "He confirmed a connection between himself and the knife. I'm amazed."

The inspector replies, "We've got enough…the connections all line up. He's connected to the knife…and the knife connects him to two murders, his father and Patricia. We need a motive for Patricia's murder and for the Larry Musgrove murder…Not that we have his motive for murdering his father, but it's usually someone close, and the closer the more likely. We've got work to do. We'll figure out the motives, fill in the gaps and connect all the pieces."

"But it's not nearly complete. His wife's missing? There's no connection to the Musgrove murder? And where is Alexander Gislason? The box of stuff was found at his place. He's definitely connected to this, for sure."

Williams replies, "What we have is a box of stuff we retrieved from where we picked up Oddleifson. He likely planted it there."

"What're you thinking here?"

Inspector Williams leans back in his chair. "Look at the whole thing. This guy's a mystery writer. He thinks this way. He lays out clues that knit together, forming an airtight case against his target. It's very possible, I think most likely he's behind all of this."

"Target? Who could he be targeting?"

192

"The target's the half-brother Gislason. With Oddleifson as the perp everything falls into place. Most likely he wrote 'The Bastard' on his own window, to plant evidence of someone being after him."

"You're right, it seems like everything points to him, but I know him. He's not a murderer. He's smart and creative. He cares about this community and people. He's moved back here to his home town, fell in love, married, settled in. He's not a murderer."

The inspector sits up straighter and continues, "Look at the number of things that are obviously linked to Oddleifson: the raccoon, Larry Musgrove's corpse in his car trunk, his wife missing, the knife linking him to his father's murder and Patricia's murder. And he admits having it at one time. I think we've got our suspect. I hear your objection, but for me the evidence is overwhelming. You watch, as we fill in the gaps it'll become clearer that he's our man. We don't have motives yet, but do wackos need motives?"

Sergeant Phillips sits back, rubs his chin and tips his head slightly. "Could Susie Oddleifson's background be part of her disappearance?"

"That is a possibility. Susie has quite a background. She entered Canada under a false ID and it was her testimony that put the leadership of Rumble Riot on death row. They have a long memory and if they come back to Gimli she'll be the reason."

"We get regular updates on Rumble Riot movements and there's no indication they're near here."

"Yes. But I'll have headquarters do an analysis, look for patterns in their movements."

193

The sergeant looks at the inspector. "So we have Rumble Riot and Steve Oddleifson as suspects in Susie's abduction. How should we proceed?"

"We'll focus on Oddliefson as our prime suspect. A phone tap for sure, and surveillance. As I said, I'll request an updated analysis from headquarters on the Riot's movements. But in the meantime we'll review everything with Steve as the likely perpetrator. We have to build the evidence into a solid case."

Irving sits in the arm chair facing Steve on the couch. He finger combs his hair and each strand falls obediently back into place. He takes a breath and says to Steve, "You might think they were after information about Susie, but I think they're looking at you as a suspect."

"How the hell…"

"The contents of the box have nothing to do with Susie. They were focusing on you, not her."

"Good God. So, what…what should we do?"

"First of all, you're not going back there for questioning unless they arrest you."

"What! Arrest me? What for?"

"We've got a long list of crimes, take your pick."

"Do you really think I'm in trouble?" Steve's eyebrows raise.

"Yes and I'm assigning a bodyguard to you."

"Why? Why do that?"

"First of all, I want a witness to everything you do from now on. And I want you to stop running off and messing up evidence that might help you. You need a babysitter."

194

Chapter Thirty-Three — The Hunting Shack

Saturday 7 AM

Susie opens one eye a slit. *What's that smell? Where am I?* She looks over at Alexander. *He's sleeping...and I fell asleep, didn't want that. God, what is on top of me, it stinks! Musty and God knows what else. An old sleeping bag?...I'm starving. Pizza boxes, well, he ate. Who the hell is he? What's he want?* She pulls on her wrist and the twine digs in. *Oooo!* She strains to look up at the headboard. Alex moves and Susie shuts her eyes. *Okay, still sleeping, be silent, stay alive, stay alive...every moment counts...don't rile him...calm...* Standing now, Alex steps over to the bed and nudges her leg. Susie's mind flashes to Rumble Riot...sweaty bikers, rape, crushing weight, beer breath, thrown...she remembers thinking, *my god, I'm going to die,* and her eyes fill with tears. He nudges her again. "Wake up, my Angel Sigga," he says in a quiet voice.

She snaps back to the present. *Okay it's now or never.* She inhales deeply as if she's just awakening and flutters her eyes open. She pulls her arms and feigns surprise at being tied to the headboard. *He calls me his 'angel', he probably wants me to be okay...* She pretends to struggle, just a bit, then, remaining silent, puts a dejected, defeated look on her face, lets her body slump into the bed. She slowly looks up at him and asks, "Who are you? Why am I tied here?" *Be a person, smile...* She manages a smile.

Alexander frowns and looks down at her. *She's smiling. My Angel is smiling at me.* His face relaxes and he opens his mouth but nothing comes out. Frustrated, he groans.

195

Susie asks again, "Who are you?"

Surprised, Alex looks at her and walks away. He sits down in the overstuffed chair and stares. *My Angel doesn't know me.* ***Of course she doesn't know you, you fool. What an idiot!*** "Shut the fuck up mother!"

Startled, Susie cringes. *Does he think I'm his mother? He's seriously crazy...go slowly. Very slowly.* "Please tell me your name."

Alex looks at her suspiciously and hesitates.

She repeats, "Please."

"It's Alex."

"Hi Alex. I really need to go to the bathroom."

"Er, bathroom. Do you promise not to run away?"

"Yes I promise."

Alex unties her hands from the headboard and tells her to stand up. He ties the twine around her waist. "The bathroom's outside." As they walk, Susie breathes in the cool autumn air and looks around for any sign of life. *Okay, one truck, nothing but brush, no houses, no roads.* Alex pulls her tether and leads her around the back to a ramshackle outhouse. He steps in, tests the floor and clears the spider webs with his arm, steps back out and nods at her to go in.

Susie closes the door with the twine running through the gap below the door. Her eyes adjust to the darkness. She sits and pees, all the while thinking, *Okay, seems he's not gonna hurt me. He thinks he knows me, no, Sigga, he knows Sigga. Where's this headed? What's he want? Why'd he abduct me? No, why'd he abduct Sigga?* Finished, she opens the door. Alex is standing, holding the line.

"Back inside." He turns and leads her off.

Susie obediently walks behind him, down the trampled path to the door and steps in. *I have to keep him talking. Gain his trust.* "Could I have some pizza?"

"Of course, you're my Angel Sigga." Alexander stands awkwardly holding the line. He says to himself, *Now what do I do? Take her with me to get the pizza? No, I'll tie her to something.* "Sit at the table." He ties the line to the chair leg, says, "I'll get pizza," and steps outside.

Susie sits quietly. *What's going on? I've got to get him talking.*

Alex steps back in with a pizza box and a two litre coke. *Good, she hasn't moved. Maybe I can trust her a bit.* "Pizza's all we got but we've got lots of it." He smiles at his own joke.

He's joking... "Good one." She smiles and chuckles. "Pizza, my favourite."

Alex opens the box, takes two pieces and sits in the overstuffed chair. "Dig in. That coke's yours."

"Thanks for clearing the spiders from the outhouse. I hate spiders. You're my hero."

Alex jerks his head up from his pizza. *Hero! I'm her hero...or is she playing me?* "It wasn't heroic."

"Well, I think you were brave. I couldn't have scared them away and you did. So I'll think of you as my hero."

"Okay, I'll be your hero." Alex sits a little straighter in the chair. *I like that. I'm my Angel Sigga's hero, yeah.*

Most of the pizza and half the coke are gone and Susie relaxes back in her chair. "Alex?" His head snaps towards her. "I need to go to the bathroom again. Do you mind?"

Once again Alex stands outside the outhouse holding the tether traveling through the gap at the door bottom. Long finished, Susie pushes the door open. She smiles at Alex and says, "Thanks, that was very necessary." Alex looks lovingly

197

at her and still holding the twine, follows her back into the shack.

He looks like he's in love...Yes, he loves Sigga. How can I use this?

She sits on the bed. "Thanks for letting me go to the bathroom."

Alex smiles. "More pizza?"

"No, I feel full and happy."

Alex sits in his chair without tying the twine to the bed.

Susie wonders, *Did he forget? Better not say anything. Keep him talking.* She picks up the twine, walks over and sits back at the table. She coils it carefully and puts it on the table in front of herself. "Alex, what's your last name?"

He looks confused. "Don't you remember? Gislason, my last name's Gislason."

Susie tries to look calm. *Good grief, could it be...oh God...Jerry, yeah Jerry Erikson, at our party...I'm sure Jerry said the fisherman out on the lake was Gislason, yeah, Alex Gislason. What in the world's happening here? What does he want with me...no...with Sigga?* She slowly asks, "Sorry, I'm confused. When did we meet?"

Alex becomes agitated. "What? You know...Is this a game?...You must know. You were going into the church for your Afi's funeral. You wore a blue dress." A faraway look softens his face. "You were an angel, my Angel..." He snaps back to reality. *No, that's wrong... she didn't even look at me...what the hell am I thinking...**Bad, you're bad, you're a bad boy...*** Alex sucks in a breath and yells, "Get out of my head you fucking bitch." ***Bad, Bad, you're a bad little boy...*** "Fuck off Mother. I'm with my Angel, my Angel Sigga and you're dead. I watched you die, remember?"

He really is nuts…and I'd better be Sigga, his Angel…
"So you saw me that day. I was with my mother, were you with your family?"

"Yes…" Alex's eyes glaze over as he remembers sitting on the grass across the street watching them enter the church. He remembers the pain as he watched his father put his arm on Steve's shoulder. Then he frowns and shakes his head. "Sorta…My dad was there." *I wanted him to see me. I just wanted my dad to look at me.* Alex's face falls and he begins to sob.

Oh dear God what did I say? Quick, think fast Susie. "Who's your dad? I probably know him."

Alex looks at her, stops sobbing and laughs. "Of course you know him. You were there. Right beside him. My dad, Richard Oddleifson."

Susie controls her face as this piece of the puzzle falls into place. *This guy's Steve's brother! Keep him talking.*

"And your mother, was she there?"

Mother, my mommy. "I watched her die. She's dead."

"Was she at the funeral?"

"She was jammed in the couch, couldn't breathe, she died." His face screws up. "She died and I watched her, she died." A look of terror floats onto his face. He stands and runs from the house, bends forward in the tall grass and retches.

Susie grabs the coil of twine and runs out behind him. "Did you try to save her?"

"I screamed at her…she screamed, she always screams at me. I screamed back at her…She's dead. She died and I watched her and I'm glad." He collapses to his knees, sobbing.

I've hit a nerve. "Did you try to save her?"

199

Surprised, wide-eyed he says, "No," he thinks for a second, "I always loved mommy. I love her…Mommy why don't you love me. I'm just a little boy. I love you Mommy. I love you." He sobs into his hands.

"Why did you bring me here?'

From his knees Alex parts his hands and looks up. "You're my Angel Sigga, I love you, you're mine. We live together now. We'll be happy together without Steve."

"Do you remember Steve from school?"

"That bastard got everything. I got nothing. He's my brother and I got nothing." His face hardens. "He's gonna pay, pay big."

He's the one! He scrawled 'bastard' on the window. "Is that why you wrote 'U R the bastard' on Steve's window?"

Becoming suspicious, Alex stands and looks closely at Susie, then cautiously answers, "Yes, that's why. He's the real bastard, not me. I was born first."

I'll bet it's all him. "And the raccoon. Did you do that wonderful raccoon?"

The word 'wonderful' relaxes Alex. He smiles and replies, "Yes, wasn't it great?"

"Yeah, that was the best. And Larry Musgrove, did you know him? Was it you who put him in the trunk? That was excellent."

Alex bends forward, grabs his face and moans. Tears flow through his fingers. "I didn't mean to…he wouldn't shut up… I didn't mean to…"

"I think you should lie down for a while. You've done a lot of hard things and you need rest. Lie down now. Come with me." He stands, hunched in a sobbing stupor. He appears to shrink as Susie leads him obediently back into the shack. She takes his hand and leads him to the bed.

He lies down and looks lovingly up at her. He turns onto his side, draws his knees up and wraps his arms around them. He buries his face in his arms and sobbing, says quietly, "Hug me Joe, be my friend, I'm just a little boy, love me, hug me."

Good God. Who the hell's Joe? Susie shakes her head as she unties the rope from her waist. *Another person he's killed?*

He cuddles his knees, closes his eyes and continues whimpering.

Susie's mouth falls open. *The fetal position! He's totally regressed, he is a little boy…Truck keys, where…*

She gently slides her hand into his yawning pant pocket. *Success!* Not breathing, she walks backwards to the door, turns, runs out, jumps in the truck and inserts the key. The truck roars to life. The pedals are too far but she wedges herself forward and pushes down the clutch, shifts to first and gives it gas. The truck lurches forward. She turns the wheel sharply only to stop suddenly against something hidden in the grass. She depresses the clutch again and her door flies opens. "You said you wouldn't leave. You promised."

My God, think Susie! "Thank God you're okay. I was going for help."

"I don't believe you. You were leaving. Everyone leaves me. You promised." Alex's face hardens. He pulls her from the truck. His fingers dig into Susie's upper arm. She winces. Alex yells, "You promised you would stay with me. You lied."

Desperate, Susie says, "No Alex, I was getting help. I was so worried about you."

In his mother's 'you're bad' voice Alex says, "I don't believe you. You promised…"

Susie reaches up and strokes his face. "I'll never leave you. I promise. It's just you and me. Let's go back and have some pizza. You want some pizza now."

201

His face softens at Susie's touch and he wavers. "You promised me..."

"I promise. I will never leave you. Let's go back in and have more pizza. I'm hungry. You like pizza, right?"

"Yeah, pizza." Still suspicious but enthralled by her touch, his hold on her arm loosens and then he lets go. Susie, sensing an opening, takes hold of his hand. *Her hand, so soft...she loves me.* He smiles and turns back towards the shack.

Pizza crusts litter the bed and darkness has blackened the windows. Susie feigns a yawn and says, "I'm really tired. I want to sleep."

"You sleep here. I'll sleep in the chair." He stands and pushes the chair in front of the door and sits down. Susie lies back on the crust strewn bed and pretends to sleep. *Alright, he hasn't tied me to anything. I could grab that iron doorstop and be out a window in a flash...but he'd probably grab me as quick. Tomorrow's another day...I'll get out of this mess tomorrow.*

Chapter Thirty-Four — Steve and Oscar

Saturday Morning 7:30 AM

Steve half opens an eye and tries to orient himself. *What the hell?* He reaches out but instead of the silkiness of his sheet he finds the rougher sofa fabric. *God, I'm sleeping in the living room!* He looks at his watch. *7:30…least I got a couple hours.* He snaps awake, says out loud, "Susie. My God, Susie. Gotta find Susie." He jumps up, runs, grabs his jacket, yanks the door open and stops, stunned.

A bald man holding two grocery bags stands poised to ring the bell. His duffel sits on the porch beside him. Focusing, Steve says hesitantly, "Who are…," but recognition is instant when the man looks slightly to the right, the missing top of his left ear, the scar. "Ah, Oscar..." *Irving's gangster chef.*

"Yeah, Spellman sent me. You look like hell, man. Where's the kitchen?" He bends down, retrieves the duffel bag and pushes past Steve.

Confused, Steve points the way to the kitchen. "Excuse me, why are you here?"

"Like I said, Spellman sent me. Where's the bedroom?"

"Bedroom?"

"Yeah, my bedroom. Are youse deaf?"

"Now wait just a minute…"

"Ah, don't get butt-hurt."

Steve looks suspiciously at him. "What're you saying?"

"Butt-hurt?" Oscar laughs. "Don't get upset, that's all man. Didn't Irving call ya?"

"No, he did not."

203

"Okay. Irving says I gotta stay witya. He don't want ya alone. Security, right? Some nut out there and ya can't be alone. Alibi right? Got it?"

Steve's brain-fog slowly clears. *Right, Irving said I needed a babysitter.* "Okay I got it." He turns and sits down on the sofa again. "You don't understand, no one understands, I have to find Susie. That maniac has her. Have to find her. God I'm tired."

"You look like hell. When'd ya sleep last?"

"I need coffee. I need to think."

"No java. I know what youse need. Ya just sit there and I'll bring ya something to drink. Relax."

Steve closes his eyes. *Yeah sure, relax. I need to get moving and find Susie. No one seems to be doing anything.* He hears Oscar opening cupboards. *Putting those damn groceries away, he should be looking for Susie not babysitting me.*

Oscar finds some baking chocolate and puts milk on to heat. He chops the chocolate and adds it to the pot. He pours in some sugar and stirs slowly while looking out the window. *This poor bastard's in rough shape. I know just what he needs.* He pours the steaming liquid into two mugs. He pulls a bottle from his duffel and selects a capsule. Carefully he pries the capsule apart, stirs the powder into one mug and heads to the living room.

"Here, get this down ya."

Steve sits up. "This isn't coffee." He pushes it away.

"Better than java ya jerk. Ya wanna stay up forever?"

"Yes I do. I have to find my wife."

"You ain't finding no one in this condition. When'd ya eat last? Chocolate's good for ya, drink up."

Steve tries to remember the last time he ate. The chocolate smells enticing. "Okay, but then I have to get going." He sips

204

and watches Oscar, sizing him up. "Where you from Oscar? You sound American."

Oscar smiles and nods. "Yeah, I been all over." He points at the cup. "Be careful it's hot." He sits down and watches him slowly drink.

"You sound like a New Yorker."

"Yeah, born in New York but I've lived all over. Now why don't you and me strategize a little…make a plan, right? Now when was the last time ya saw Susie? Let's start at the beginning. Bring me up tah speed."

Steve begins with breakfast the day before. "God she looked so sweet as she…" He sips and talks while Oscar asks the occasional question. It isn't long before he leans back and the words are coming out a little slower. Oscar takes the empty mug.

"I feel funny. What's happening…"

"You're relaxing man. Ya need to hit the sack. C'mon. Up you go." He lifts Steve to his feet and moves towards the hallway. "Which way man?"

Steve points. "Did you put something in my…?"

"Yeah, just a little somethin'. Irving and the guys are comin' over for chow later and we'll all sit down and talk."

Disoriented, Steve looks at the alarm clock. *5:00. What happened? I was talking…to Oscar?* He rolls over and looks out the window. *Still daylight. What's that smell? God it smells good. Smells like Sunday when I was a kid.* He sits up suddenly, *Susie! Oh my God, Susie!* He tries to stand but the room spins and he lies back down. *Right, he put something in the chocolate.* He groans, lowers his feet to the floor and sits, waiting for his head to clear.

Oscar appears, "Good, you're up. Here's some water and toast. Eat up. The guys'll be here soon."

"You drugged me."

Oscar smiles. "Yup."

"I need to…"

"You need tah eat that toast and take a shower. Eat, then get your ass in there and look good for your company. They're all coming tah tell us what they've found out and then we make a plan."

Reluctantly, Steve takes a bite of toast. "What's that smell?"

"Dinner." And Oscar closes the door behind himself.

Steve, freshly showered, shaved and dressed, steps into the kitchen to question Oscar, but before he can start, the doorbell rings. Oscar pushes past him and says, "I'll get it."

"I think I can answer my own door."

"Nope. That's why I'm here. Nut on the loose, remember?"

Hearing Vlad's voice, Steve rushes over. "Vlad, what do you know? Have you heard anything?"

Vlad is spared from answering by the doorbell ringing again. The two men watch as Oscar lets Irving in. Steve tries to question him but Irving holds up his hand. "Not here. Let's go into the living room. Evan's right behind me."

Steve paces back and forth. Frustrated, he says loudly, "For God's sake someone tell me something. I'm going crazy here."

Evan breezes in. "Hey guys."

Oscar comes in with a tray of glasses and a bottle of rye whiskey. He places the tray on the table and pushes Steve into a chair. "Sit."

206

Steve looks at Irving. "What the hell have you saddled me with?"

Evan interrupts, "Got some beer?"

Irving smiles. "Got any red wine Oscar? Now, Steve. We've all been busy and we have some info. Let's start with Evan. Okay?"

Before Evan can start, Oscar puts a bottle of wine and three beer on the coffee table and settles heavily on the end of the sofa. Vlad is thrown by the movement and carefully balances his glass of whiskey while glaring at Oscar. "Damn it, be careful." Oscar grins and grabs a beer.

Evan looks at Irving. "Ernie sends his regrets. They went to Edmonton with Trisha's husband. Funeral's next Saturday."

Steve groans. "Oh God, poor Jeannie. We have to stop this maniac, can't just sit here."

Evan puts up his hand. "That's why we're all here. We have to compare notes and decide what we can do. I've been quietly talking to my contacts. Everyone has clammed up. I think you're right Irving, Steve's their main suspect now." Steve stands, Evan continues, "This Alexander Gislason is a person of interest and they're looking for him but I'm pretty sure it's to eliminate him as a suspect."

Steve yells, "What? You can't be serious. Me? Why would I abduct my own wife?" He starts pacing. "Are they even looking for her?"

Vlad says, "Yes they are. I've been watching the cops. They're going door to door, trying to find anyone who saw anything around the time the car was found out on the highway. They're questioning her friends. She is officially a missing person. And they definitely suspect foul play. There's an APB out on her and Alexander. But they're also asking pointed questions about you Steve."

207

"Sit down Steve." Irving motions to him. "Let's talk about what we know."

Steve slumps back on the sofa. "We know that some maniac is trying to frame me and that he probably has Susie. We can't just sit here…"

Irving looks at Steve and says, sternly, "Yes we're going to sit here and use our brains. As I was saying, we know someone is trying to frame you. We don't know for sure who, but the evidence we've dug up concerning this Gislason makes him our prime suspect. The police have the knife that killed Trisha and the forensic testing reveals it killed your father as well, Steve. Alex might have killed his own father and could hate you enough to try and make you pay for it."

Evan says, "I agree," and looks at Vlad, who nods.

Steve looks helplessly at his friends. "We need to find him. I'm sure he has Susie. And sitting here isn't getting us anywhere. She's out there with a maniac."

Irving says, "Steve, you are not to leave this house without one of us. You have to be protected, both from this maniac and, I'm sorry to say, from the police."

Frustrated, Steve pours a glass of whiskey and empties it in one gulp. "I can't just sit here."

"No, your job is to find out everything you can about your father. He's a major link between you and Gislason. Do you still have any of his effects? Are there any other family members still around?"

"I don't know. We've moved several times. And now this move here…Let me think." He pours another drink. Vlad, worried, looks at Steve and moves the whiskey bottle further down the table, just out of reach.

"Okay. As I said, Steve your job is to research your family and any family artifacts available. Evan, you keep talking

208

with your contacts. Nothing wrong with dropping 'Gislason' into any conversation. Vlad, continue monitoring police activity...and your profiling work with Marion is proving valuable. Make sure she's up to date with how we're proceeding. I'm going to make my presence known at the detachments...both here and Winnipeg. And all of us will focus on this Gislason."

A timer goes off in the kitchen and Oscar stands. "Grub's on."

Steve tries to stand. Vlad gives him a hand and they head towards the dining room table. "Sure smells good Oscar. What're we having?"

"Beef Bourguignon. Beef stew to youse bums."

Chapter Thirty-Five — Marion and Irving

Sunday Morning – Gimli Community Health Centre

Douglas shifts in what they called a comfortable armchair. *I wonder if they have uncomfortable ones.* He looks out the hospital room window at the houses across the street. *Gimli, Sunday morning, is there anything more peaceful?* Marion stirs and he gives her his total attention. "Good morning sleepyhead." He bends over her and kisses her forehead.

Marion smiles sleepily, "You call that a kiss?" She grabs his shirt front and pulls him in, gives him a 'Congratulations! You're a Father!' kiss.

He straightens up, very awake. "Now that was a kiss, thanks. You're obviously recovering, fast...our baby looks great. They're bathing him. I watched for a while. He's just amazing. You're amazing."

She looks over at the baby's empty cot. "How long 'til he's back?"

"About ten minutes."

Marion checks her watch. "That'll be long enough. One quick call. Hand me my purse."

He hesitantly passes it to her. "You might not think it, but you do need rest. Your blood pressure's elevated. That's why you haven't been released. Rest and we could go home today. You made, what, half a dozen calls to Vlad yesterday. And it wore you out...not to mention you got almost nothing."

"Don't worry, I'm not calling Vlad. I know I have to stay calm, but it's stressful not knowing anything. Some information will calm me down, I promise, trust me." She rummages in her purse. "I'm going to call Irving, he'll know

210

what's happening." With a pleased look she pulls out a small book and flips through the pages, calls Irving, waits, then dives into conversation.

"Hello Irving. It's Marion. What's developed?"

"Marion. How are you? How's the baby?"

"We're fine, both of us fine. Well, I kind of have a blood pressure thingy but it's good, really, I'm good. I need to know what's going on."

Blood pressure. I better not tell her about Susie. "Nothing important yet. You should be resting. Don't worry, everything's being taken care of. You need rest."

"They're bringing the baby to me in a few minutes. Please, just a quick update. I promise to rest. And Douglas's here. He doesn't let me get away with much."

"Okay, the short version. As you know, RCMP forensics takes time. Everything they produce has to be bullet-proof for court presentation, but…a bit has come through."

"Quit torturing me. Spill it."

"Sorry, Vlad said he told you about the Boy Scout knife and Richard Oddleifson's murder. Even though they have his blood on the knife, that doesn't conclusively identify the knife as the murder weapon. But he did die from a knife wound to the jugular and blood was wiped on Richard's sleeve. The width of that wipe is consistent with a smaller knife like the Boy Scout jack-knife, but again, nothing conclusive. What is for sure is that the knife has Richard's blood on it and because of that, most likely it was used to murder him."

"What else?"

"Larry Musgrove's single wound was not made by the jack-knife, but it was clearly the weapon used for Trisha's murder. There were no usable prints on the knife, but other matter is packed into the jack-knife joints and the bone handle...could be just dirt."

"So there's no link established yet between Gislason and the Boy Scout knife...Anything from Trisha's crime scene?"

"There's a foot print behind a bush where they think the perp hid and it matches the size of a foot print leaving Richard's murder. Again, nothing conclusive. Of course everyone has been thoroughly interviewed and the scene has been scoured. The forensic autopsy of Trisha's body has been completed but there's no report available."

Marion says, "I'm focusing on Alex Gislason's life. I got that buffet from Mrs Finnson and she said Alex's mother Ruby died tragically in the early '60's and that Alex was placed in care. Vlad told me Alex's father Richard was murdered in 1966. The documents found in the buffet indicate that just before that murder Alex turned twenty-one and he would have received a trust fund from his mother's estate."

"So, where can research into his life lead? What conclusions could come out of this?"

"The posing of the eviscerated raccoon corpse and the staging of Larry Musgrove's body both indicate a traumatic event in the perp's life. So far we've got two potential events, Richard's murder and Ruby's death. Losing a parent is a life-altering trauma, but I'm looking for a close, personal involvement in one of these events. And then, according to profiling theory, he'd be trying to fix, or balance the world to make things right."

Irving says, "That fits."

"Fits what?"

"I've been talking with Phillips from Gimli RCMP. He has a minor indicator that Alex could have been involved in Ruby's death."

"What?…Minor?…That's huge!"

"Yes, now I understand that it could be very significant, but the indicator is still minor. It's an obscure note in the attending officer's notebook."

"You have a copy?"

"No, Phillips wouldn't go that far, but he read it to me. If it's needed we could subpoena it."

"Can we find the officer?"

"Unfortunately he's passed on."

"Do you remember what was written?"

"I made a note: the officer was standing in the living room and wrote…son Alexander was silent, relaxed and happy, seemed proud…And that's all Phillips thought worthy of reading. Phillips was stopped by the word 'proud'."

"Wow! If he was proud of her death, that's likely the trauma. Then Richard's murder would be after the initial trauma. Maybe, if we can link the knife…"

Irving cautions, "Hold on, don't go jumping to conclusions. 'Proud' can't be seen. It has to be a feeling the officer had. Who knows if he was right? All we have is a reaction that Phillips had about one word in a twenty year old note book. But it does generate a question: What could young Alex have been smiling and happy about?…And even if the officer was correct and he was proud of something, it doesn't mean he was involved in her death."

"Okay, okay. I guess I'm moving too fast. Was there anything else? From the RCMP analysis I mean."

"They've gathered a truck load of material from the fish processing shack. And that'll take a few more days before even preliminary info is available. They're still at the house and yard. They've not been able to locate Gislason's truck. At present the RCMP say the crimes are being treated as

213

separate. This doesn't make sense if you look at the amount of time and effort being put into each situation. This indicates they're holding back info. But I think you're right — we should look at their shared history and at the Boy Scout knife. Finding the connections will focus our hunt."

"Yes, the knife can link it all together, but my focus is trauma in Alex's early life. I feel the Gislason, Steve and Richard Oddleifson trio, their lives and interactions is where the key is. If we can find that key, we'll understand what's happening and I think everything'll be clear."

"Maybe Steve can remember or dig up some stuff. Think of any other sources?" Irving adds.

"The treasure trove, I mean the cigar box of souvenirs that Steve found. Any information about that?"

"Yes, they're now calling them 'souvenirs' as well. Steve was able to identify many of the items, except for a few, such as a blue earring. And there's a man's wedding ring. Steve thinks it might be his father's."

"My God...was there anything else he couldn't ID?"

"There were items they didn't even ask him about...such as a piece of cloth, likely a shirt collar...stuff like that. Nothing significant."

"This could be the trophy collection of a serial killer. Everything's significant. How can I get a complete list of the box contents?"

"I'll ask. But I doubt you'll get an answer soon. What're you thinking?"

"The earring could have been his mother's...and if the wedding ring was his father's...then they might be trophies connected to those events. The reason the Boy Scout knife wasn't in the box is it was in Trisha's gut. It's as simple as that."

214

Irving pauses then says, "So the treasure box could be central."

"Yes, central…linking the knife to the box could be as important as linking it to Alex directly."

A nurse holding a small bundle appears at the room door.

"And here's my baby! Gotta go. Thanks for the update."

Marion tries to hand the phone back, but Douglas is already cuddling their son.

She smiles and leans back, "Our son."

Chapter Thirty-Six — The Photograph

Sunday Morning – Steve and Susie Oddleifson's Home

Steve opens one eye, his brain screams. *Arggh!* He tenderly holds his head and tries to piece together the origin of his blinding headache. *Oscar...dinner...did my keeper drug me again?* He groans as the pieces fall into place. *All that rye, ow, maybe quite a bit of red wine...Susie!* He sits up quickly, too quickly, his head pounds, the room spins. *God, I have to find Susie.* He stands cautiously, wavers, the room slowly tilts back to normal. *Cold shower, that'll wake me up, then Susie. Got to find Susie.*

In the shower his memory of the evening clears. *Right. Irving gave us all jobs. I've got to find Dad's stuff. Search for clues. Got to be something there. My so-called brother has to be at the bottom of this mess. Where the hell has that bastard taken her...Dad, what have you done?*

Dressed, he walks slowly out to the kitchen. *I smell coffee, I need coffee.*

Oscar turns. "Morning, Sunshine. Ready to get to work?"

Steve heads straight for the coffee machine. "First coffee...got a cure for a hell of a hangover?"

Oscar laughs. "Water, water and then some more water. Sorry."

Steve takes his coffee over to the sofa. "Okay. Give me a minute."

"Sure thing boss. Want something to eat?"

"God no!"

216

Steve takes a tentative sip and sits back. "Have you heard anything?"

"Nope."

"Damn." *Okay Dad's stuff then. Where did I put those boxes? Office? Maybe garage.*

Oscar sits opposite him and says, "Gotta plan?"

"Yes, find my dad's boxes. I have a couple of them somewhere here. Been carrying them around with me for a long time. Never really looked at them. "

"Well let's get started. Unless ya want somethin' ta eat...?"

Steve shakes his head, winces with the motion. "God no."

"Okay then where do we start?"

"I have some boxes in a storage area in the garage rafters. May as well start there."

Half an hour later, Oscar hands down a box marked 'Arlene'..."Who's Arlene?"

"My wife. Deceased."

"Oh, sorry man."

"No problem. Long time ago." Steve looks around at the boxes scattered around the garage floor. Some plainly labeled but others half opened to identify the contents. "Are there many more?"

"Against the rafters...wait a sec..." Oscar moves further into the eaves and yells, "two more, hold on. Yup, can't see what they say." He hands them down and steps back onto the ladder.

"This is it. See, 'Mom and Dad'. Thank goodness."

"Ya wanna put these others back?"

"No, later. Right now I want to look through these."

"So far this box is mostly Mom." Steve looks up exasperated. He is about to push it away and open the other, but Oscar stops him. "Finish it man. Youse don't wanna miss nothing."

"Okay, okay." He continues pulling out the contents. "Pictures, letters, certificates, poems, I'll look at these letters…but later. Look at these pictures. God I loved this bike." He passes it to Oscar. "My pride and joy."

"Wow, great bike. Lucky kid. Wish I'd had a bike like that."

"It was cool. Boy was Dad mad at me when he ran over it. Got grounded for a week. Big lecture on taking care of my stuff." Steve shakes his head. "You know, I always took care of my stuff. And I know I put that bike away. You know if that bastard stole my other stuff maybe he moved my bike too. That bastard! If I could get my hands on him right now… I'd…I'd kill him."

"Nah…killin's too easy, man. Ya wanna make 'im suffer. Killing's too quick."

"You may have a point. Something to think about." And Steve continues to look at each item he pulls out of his Mom's box. "Done. Now for Dad."

Steve pulls item after item from the box and thinks out loud, "If that birth certificate is genuine and Gislason's my brother, that means Dad was carrying on for many years with another woman. It makes no sense. I swear my mom and dad were happy. What was he thinking? What kind of man was he? I feel like I didn't know my own Dad."

Oscar looks at Steve. "Ya know man, ya really don't know about other people. Even your dad was a person with a life youse'll never know about." He hesitates a moment, "Take me for instance. Ya don't know anything 'bout me. I could be a killer…a rapist…many bad things. We all got secrets."

218

Steve laughs. "Right. A killer. C'mon."

"Yup. A killer. Ever killed anyone Steve?"

"Of course not."

"Well I have. See, ya don't know everything about a person. So cut your dad some slack. He lived his life and you're livin' yours. Like I say, we all got secrets."

Surprised, Steve looks at Oscar. "Okay. What's your story anyway?"

"I'm not ashamed of my past. I was in the Army and ya did what ya had to do."

"Oh, war and all that, right?"

Oscar smiles, "Ever hear of CANSOCOM?"

Steve shakes his head. "Canso...what?"

"CANSOCOM, Canadian Special Operations Command."

"Wow. You're kidding me."

"Nope. And that's why I say ya can never really know anyone. And that's all I'm saying. So let's get back to business here. What's in the box?"

"Right, box." Still digesting what he's been told, he looks at Oscar, *that's a killer?* Oscar points at the box.

"Susie, remember?"

Steve shuffles through picture after picture and stops at one and stares at it. "Here's one of my grandfather and my father as a young kid. Look at my Granddad's getup. They really went all out when they hunted." He passes the picture to Oscar. A middle age gentleman and a teenage boy are standing in front of a shack, each holding a rifle. The grandfather is decked out in short plaid pants tucked into knee high stockings and finished off with leather boots and a fedora. Oscar chuckles and hands it back.

"Quite the stylish gent."

219

Steve stares at the picture. "You know…I think I know this place." He sits back and his brow furrows. *Why do I remember that place?*

"Are youse ready for some food yet?"

Lost in thought Steve mumbles, "Uh, food…right. Maybe. Yeah, okay, food."

Oscar leaves and yells back at Steve, "Is a sandwich good or do ya want toast?"

Getting no response, Oscar steps out of the kitchen. "Steve. Sandwich or toast?"

"Toast."

From the fridge Oscar hears Steve shout, "I know this place. This is the hunting shack my dad took me too…He was having an affair, he'd need privacy. I bet he went there with her, yeah, that makes sense. She would have known about the shack, most likely Gislason got there at some time. Gislason needs privacy now…that's it, that's where he is…" Steve stands and sucks in a breath, grabs his keys from the hall table and bolts out the door.

Oscar is close behind. He grabs the passenger door and slides in as Steve hits the accelerator. "Hey. Ya go nowhere without me. Remember. What the hell's up?"

"I know that shack. That hunting shack. My dad took me there, lots of times. I just know that's where he has Susie."

"You can't know that. Maybe it's a hunch."

"Well it's a hunch I'm checking out. Hold on." The car leans out of the driveway and presses Oscar back in the seat as it accelerates.

Chapter Thirty-Seven — The Chase

Constable Warren is bored. His unmarked car is positioned to provide clear sight lines to the Oddleifson house. There has been activity entering and leaving the house but Oddleifson has not left the premises for a day and a half. He sighs, puts his coffee in the cup holder and unwraps his Robin's doughnut. The jam oozes out onto his chin. "Shit." He reaches for the napkin. He catches the drip just in time and looks back to the house to see the garage door open. Steve's Corvette roars out of his driveway and smokes rubber down Lake Street.

"Holy Crap!" Warren drops the doughnut, switches on the ignition, floors the cruiser and fishtails after him. He gains control and punches the radio. "Karen patch me through to Phillips now!"

The desk clerk fumbles with the headset, focuses, then completes the connection. The line rings, rings...long seconds pass, then Sergeant Phillips asks, "Warren what's going on?"

"Sir, Oddleifson just left Loni in his Corvette, heading out of town on 231. He's speeding. I could..."

"No, do not apprehend, repeat, do not apprehend. Maintain a distance and see where he goes. He could lead us right to his wife."

"He's driving dangerously Sir. Could be..."

"Never mind. Just don't lose him. Keep the desk informed. I'll organize a backup detail. Do nothing. Just report his location and we'll be right behind you. Got it?"

"Yes Sir!"

Steve speeds through the stop sign at Highway 9 in front of a blue minivan. Panicked, the van driver screeches to a halt, blocking the intersection. Constable Warren slams on his brakes, curses. As the intersection clears, two cars approaching from the south make a left turn in front of him. He waits impatiently, *I need the siren....shit!* Finally the intersection clears and he speeds past both cars. His cruiser winds up to 160kph. At Highway 8 he catches sight of the Corvette speeding past Aspen Park. "Whew, there he is."

The Corvette picks up speed. Warren's speedometer slips past 170kph. The fall foliage is a blur of orange and yellow. He breathes deeply and wonders, *Where's this guy going?* The two cars fly past the industrial park and Warren thinks out loud, "Fraserwood maybe?"

A few kilometres past the air base the Corvette suddenly brakes. Warren responds, decelerating, closing the distance. Steve executes a tire scrubbing turn north onto Burma Road. Apprehensive, Warren watches the Corvette fishtail, rear tires gnawing at the edge of the ditch. "He's gonna roll!" The car recovers and speeds off. Warren releases his breath and follows the cloud of dust. He engages the radio, "Karen..." Phillips comes on right away. "Warren where are you?"

"Sir, Oddleifson has just turned north on Burma Road, I'm following."

"Good. I'm with a detail on the road, we're right behind you, keep us informed."

"Copy that."

Warren keeps the dust cloud in sight and is relieved that Oddleifson has slowed down considerably. He continues, matching his speed. The dust dissipates as the Corvette brakes, manoeuvres a 'U' turn on the narrow road and heads back towards him.

"Shit. He's heading back this way." He squeezes his radio mic, "Karen, tell Phillips to stay on 231. Oddleifson has turned around."

"I'm patching you through." The radio goes silent for a second.

"Warren. It's Phillips."

"Oddleifson is heading back towards 231. Don't enter Burma Road. I'll have to see what he's up to."

"Copy. I'll keep this line open."

Steve's Corvette passes him. He completes his own 'U' turn and follows south on Burma. Warren has the car in sight in time to see him do another 'U' turn. *Jeez Louise. What the heck's he doing*? He grabs his mic, "Sir, he's turned around again and is heading north on Burma. There's no way he doesn't make me now. What should I do?"

"Stay with him. Do not lose him. He's obviously looking for something. When he's found it let me know. We're approaching Burma Road now."

"Copy that."

Chapter Thirty-Eight — Susie, Alex, Steve and Oscar

"This's gotta be it." Steve pulls far enough over to tip the Corvette slightly into the ditch.

Oscar says, "What? I don't see anything." He looks at Steve and shakes his head. "I'm starting to…"

"No, look. This area is a little higher than the ditch. Could be an old access road. Doesn't that look like fresh tracks?"

Oscar steps out of the car, stoops down. "You're right, these are fresh. Too big for a car, maybe a truck." He points at a weakening in the low wall of scrub willow on the far side of the ditch, "went through there."

"Let's go." Steve strides purposefully towards the raised area.

"Hold back. Too much we don't know."

"Like what?" He keeps walking.

"The cops are right behind us."

Steve stops and looks at Oscar. "How the hell you know that?"

"I know cop cars, that car that passed twice was a cop. They're comin'."

"Great. At least they'll be here when we need them. Let's get in there." He starts walking again.

"It'd be better to wait." Steve continues walking. *Okay, he's determined.* He shrugs and follows.

The path is clearly marked by broken willow. Steve hunches down and pushes his way through the branches.

Oscar catches up but stops. "Steve, look here." He points at a tire track pressing grass into hard earth. "It's a truck alright and this is very fresh. I think you might be right, this might be where they're at."

Steve bolts down the road.

Oscar yells, "Wha…Wait. Hold up. Hey, Steve. Look there."

Steve stops and looks where he's pointing. He can see a vague shape through the trees.

Oscar says, "A truck. This could be it. Let's go slow."

Ignoring him, Steve tears down the overgrown road.

Oscar runs after him, whispering loudly, "Steve, stop, argh!" He hits the ground, hard. Stunned, for a second he's disoriented, then his leg jolts with pain. He tries to get up but his screaming leg is stuck. *What, a hole? Shit! Broken?* He feels his shin bone. *Damn.*

Susie sits on the bed in silence watching Alex. *He really is crazy. He sits there talking to his mother and someone named Joe. When he talks to his mother his face is so ugly but when he talks to Joe he looks like a little boy, a lost little boy.* Susie laughs and quickly swallows the laugh. *I might be getting a little crazy myself. God. A lost little boy? Get a grip...Look at him, he just sits. What's he doing? I'm worn out trying to figure out how to play this. It's been two nights…outhouse, pizza, sit, sleep…is there a plan? Where's this going?* Alexander sits in his chair hugging himself, then flings his arms violently, launching bits of stuffing from the ancient chair. *One minute he's wild, screaming at his mother and then he's meek, begging Joe to hold him. Joe? I wonder who Joe is?* Alex stops and then stares blankly at Susie on the bed.

Susie thinks, *I've gotta figure this out…* She keeps her face neutral, expressionless, lest Alex think something is needed. *It's been two days and I know things are happening*

225

out there. They've got to be searching. I hope Steve's okay... God I miss him. Alex shifts in his chair, Susie remains still. Behind Alex she sees some movement at the window. *What's that? Don't react.* Steve's face peers in the window. Susie coughs to distract.

Concerned, Alex stands and moves towards Susie. "What's wrong? Do you need any..."

Steve bursts through the door and lunges at Alex who turns, pulls back his fist, connects and Steve hits the floor, stunned, blood gushing from his nose. Alex looks around, steps to the door and picks up the iron doorstop. Steve rolls over and Alex lifts his weapon. "You're dead you bastard. I win. I win everything." He laughs manically.

"Damn you, you're the bastard!" Steve yells.

Alex bends over and yells into Steve's face, "Bastard? Bastard! You damn bastard. You took everything. You took my dad. You took my life." Alex, his face distorted, stands tall, raises the door stop high over Steve. He sucks in a breath, his eyes grow large.

Susie springs up and tackles his arm. He's surprised, staggers off balance, trips on his own feet and falls full length, the door stop smashes to the floor.

Steve jumps on his prone body but Alex rolls and straddles him. Steve looks up into the contorted face, spits out, "You're lying. You're no brother of mine. You're crazy."

Alex wraps his fingers around Steve's throat, squeezes, *This is where my hands should be...* Through grinning teeth he snarls, "You bastard. I'm going to kill you just like I killed that fucking liar of a father."

Stunned, Steve stares at him, absorbing, *killed Dad? He killed Dad.* Rage takes over. He thrusts his hand up and

226

gouges his thumb deep into Alex's right eye. Alex howls and loosens his grip. Steve throws him off and tries to stand.

Alex rolls, screams, holds his hand over his eye. His face hits the doorstop, he grabs it, staggers to his feet and reels around.

Steve raises himself up on all fours.

Alex lifts the doorstop to finish him off. Horrified, Susie throws herself at him. He falls on top of Steve. Susie hits the floor.

Steve squirms from under Alex, turns and grabs the doorstop.

Alex rolls onto Susie. *I've crushed her, my Angel. I've hurt her...*He looks into her face and says, "You alright? You okay?" Susie smells his putrid breath, feels all his weight.

Steve raises the doorstop. Susie looks up, cringes, anticipating the strike.

Alex twists, hooks Steve's legs and throws him to the floor, rolls onto him and slams his forearm into his throat. Steve tries to roll but the pressure on his throat pins him. His eyes bulge and he makes a raspy gurgling sound.

Susie grabs the doorstop, stands and lifts it with both hands. She brings it down with all her strength into the side of Alex's skull, blood sprays. Alex crumples to the floor. Susie stands looking down at him. Alex looks past her, smiles and says, "Joe, you came back." His eyes roll back and he is still.

The shack door bursts open. Phillips, Warren and three constables rush in.

227

Chapter Thirty-Nine — The Last Chapter

Sunday – late afternoon

Steve winces as the Doctor pulls the last stitch tight and ties it off. "Am I done now?"

"For now yes, but I need to examine the packing for your broken nose in a couple of days and there's still the concern of concussion so…"

Steve sits up. "Yes I know but I need to get to my wife now. Where is she?"

"She's next door being cared for. I stress the importance of…"

Steve interrupts, "Doctor I assure you I'll follow your instructions." He pats his shirt pocket, then his pants pocket, then picks up the sheet from the table beside him and holds it up. "Here it is. I will follow it to the letter. Now please, I have to see my wife."

The doctor sighs and nods but Steve is already out the door.

Susie looks up when Steve opens the examining room door. She brushes her tears away and holds out her arms. "You're here. Steve, oh my God Steve. I'm such an idiot, I can't seem to stop crying."

Steve joins her on the bed and they hold each other. "Oh Honey. Did that bastard hurt you? I was frantic not knowing where you were."

Susie kisses his forehead and says, "Shh, I'm fine. I just can't seem to stop crying. But I'm fine. He didn't hurt me. He seemed to think he was in love with me. It was so odd. He was so strange."

"Odd? He was freaking crazy. When I think what could have happened I..."

"But nothing happened. Everything's fine. But Steve, I killed him...oh my God, I killed him." Susie turns her face into Steve's shoulder and weeps.

"You saved my life Honey. Thank you. You're probably in shock. Has the Doctor given you anything?"

"They're going to give me something to take home to relax me. I've just been waiting for..." She stops and looks at the door, "Irving. It's Irving." And she starts to sob.

Irving smiles and says, "Is it okay to come in?"

Steve hurries over and pulls him into the room. "I'm so glad to see you. You won't believe everything that's happened. Come in, sit. Before I start, have you seen Oscar?"

"Yes, just came from there. His leg's broken, they're casting it as we speak. He's pretty upset that he couldn't help in the hunting shack, but he'll be fine. He told me what he knew, but please, tell me everything."

Steve sits on the bed beside Susie, holds her hand and starts the story.

Vlad holds the teddy bear tightly against his chest, wishing it fit in his pocket. He catches sight of himself in the hospital coffee shop window. *God! Shudda cleaned up a bit.* He rubs his two day stubble and quickly finger combs his hair. *Well it'll have to do. Not as if I haven't been busy.* He turns and continues down the corridor past a smirking gentleman. *Yes, it's a teddy bear. No, it's not mine. Geez.* Vlad stares him down and continues on his way to Marion's room. As he nears a set of swinging doors they burst open and Irving strides out, stops and smiles. "Just the man I'm looking for."

"Mr Spellman, Evan and I couldn't find..."

229

Irving waves his explanation away. "We missed it all. I just left Emergency...Gislason's dead. They're releasing Susie because she's fine, Steve has a broken nose and some stitches and Oscar's leg is being cast."

Mouth agape, Vlad just gets out, "What?"

Irving smiles. "I see from the teddy bear you're heading for Marion's room. Nice look by the way."

Vlad reddens behind the stubble, and Irving continues, "I'll go with you and tell you both everything. What room are they in?"

Vlad looks dazed. "109"

"Okay, let's go."

Irving peers in and sees Douglas leaning over a glowing Marion, cooing at a bundle in her arms. *A little family. So... pretty. Yes, pretty.* He clears the lump in his throat. "Ahem. Hope I'm not interrupting anything."

Marion raises a smiling face. "Irving, Vlad, come in. Come in." Douglas steps over. "I can't thank you enough for everything you did." He grasps, pumps, squeezes Irving's hand then grabs and shakes Vlad's. "Marion told me all about it. We're so lucky you were both there. Come, see our son."

Irving laughs. "Vlad deserves all the credit. Afraid I wasn't much help passed out on the floor."

Vlad blushes, walks over to Marion and extends the bear. "Here, got this in the gift shop."

Marion beams up at him and says, "Thanks Vlad, he'll love it. Look, our son, isn't he beautiful?"

Vlad peers at the little bundle and says, "He's the most beautiful boy I've ever delivered." *I'm never telling them it's been mostly calves.*

"He's so good. He's hardly cried." Marion gazes adoringly, strokes his cheek and the baby yawns. "Look

230

Honey, he's yawning." The parents are transfixed by this miracle.

"I just wanted to make sure you were okay. I met Irving in the hallway. He has something to tell us."

Marion looks over at Irving. "Sit down, both of you, and tell me everything. Is Steve okay?"

"Now Honey, you need to rest. This can all wait." Douglas looks pointedly at them.

Irving and Vlad look at each other, unsure what to do. Irving finally says, "Maybe Douglas is right. You need to rest. Think about your new baby. Everything else can wait."

"Absolutely not! Doug wants to take us home to Winnipeg tomorrow. I need to know what's happening. Now!"

They both look at Douglas.

"There's no need looking at him. I want to know and I won't get any rest until I do. Now sit down."

Vlad sighs and pulls over a chair, Irving remains standing. "Well it's quite a story. I guess I'll start with Susie's abduction."

Marion gasps. "What? No, not Susie…after everything she's gone through…what're the RCMP thinking? Do they think it's connected?"

Irving holds his hand up. "Wait, maybe I'll start at the end. Gislason is dead, and Susie, Steve and Oscar are in Emergency getting cleaned up."

Marion, bewildered now, asks, "Okay start somewhere, anywhere...what the heck has gone on?"

Irving smiles. "Well…"

Irving reaches the end and scans the stunned faces. Marion moans. "I can't believe I missed it all!"

"Um, I think you were a little busy Honey," a bemused Douglas adds.

Vlad interjects, "No wonder Evan and I could find nothing. It was all happening out of town."

Marion throws her head back in frustration. She gazes at the new life in her arms and says, "I love you little one, but did you have to come right now?" She looks up at the two men. "So it's all over? Wow! I'm so glad that it ended okay."

Irving says to Marion, "I just want to thank you for all your hard work Marion. You really did a lot of good work for this case. Without you it would have taken much longer. I can't thank you enough."

Marion smiles. "You're very welcome. But you know it helped me too. I was getting nowhere with my thesis and now with all this first hand data I have, I've lots of ideas. My mom has agreed to help me while I finish it." She looks into the tiny face in her arms. "And on time...just, I'll have you know." The three men laugh.

"Well, we have to get going, so we will leave you two, or three rather. We'll check on the injured and go find Evan."

Douglas clears his throat. "Didn't you have something you wanted to ask Vlad, Honey?"

"Oh yes. Vlad we'd like to name our boy after you. Vladimir is quite a mouthful. What's your second name?"

Vlad smiles. "Really? Well...I'm honoured. It's Afanasyev."

"Afa...what!" Marion exclaims.

"Afanasyev. A F A N A S Y E V. Just like it sounds."

Marion and Douglas look at each other, gobsmacked. Finally, Marion says, "Well, 'Vincent' it is."

Vlad starts laughing and Marion, Douglas and Irving join in. Little Vincent starts to cry.

As the other men exit the room, Irving says, "Don't cry little guy. Vincent's an excellent name." On their way to Emergency, Irving looks up at Vlad, "Now that's a nice honour." He looks closer and adds, "You're looking rough."

Vlad snorts. "I'm all out of clean clothes, except for Oscar's meal last night I haven't really eaten a decent meal in weeks and sleep? Who has had any sleep? If you don't need me I'm heading home as soon as we find Evan and fill him in."

Vlad looks Irving up and down. "How you look so good is beyond me. Even without Oscar you look all pressed and fresh…like a daisy." He laughs at his own joke.

Irving jabs him in the waist with his elbow. "Don't you get fresh." He reaches up and gives Vlad's shoulder a congratulatory pat. "You did a great job as usual. Thank you."

"That's what you pay me for."

Irving smiles. "Yes I do. I guess we have another happy ending my Russian friend."

The two men disappear behind the swinging doors.

***

www.ingramcontent.com/pod-product-compliance
Lightning Source LLC
Chambersburg PA
CBHW060053150626
46556CB00017BA/251